Grace
&
Lavender

Grace & Lavender

a novel

Heather Norman Smith

AMBASSADOR INTERNATIONAL
GREENVILLE, SOUTH CAROLINA & BELFAST, NORTHERN IRELAND

www.ambassador-international.com

Grace & Lavender

ISBN: 978-1-62020-833-5
eISBN: 978-1-62020-839-7
Library of Congress Control Number: 2019931076

Scripture taken from the New King James Version®. Copyright © 1982 by Thomas Nelson. Used by permission. All rights reserved.

Cover Design & Typesetting by Hannah Nichols
Ebook Conversion by Anna Riebe Raats
Edited by Katie Cruice Smith

AMBASSADOR INTERNATIONAL
Emerald House
411 University Ridge, Suite B14
Greenville, SC 29601, USA
www.ambassador-international.com

AMBASSADOR BOOKS
The Mount
2 Woodstock Link
Belfast, BT6 8DD, Northern Ireland, UK
www.ambassadormedia.co.uk

The colophon is a trademark of Ambassador, a Christian publishing company.

Dedication

For my daddy, always my biggest supporter

Acknowledgments

"In all your ways acknowledge Him,
And He shall direct your paths" (Prov. 3:6).
Thank you, Lord, for directing my path.

Thank you to my husband and our three children for your constant love and support. I am blessed to call you mine.

"Pure and undefiled religion before God and the Father is this:
to visit orphans and widows in their trouble,
and *to keep oneself unspotted from the world."*
(Jas. 1:27)

Chapter One

COLLEEN

COLLEEN CARTER HILL SAT AT her kitchen table with a cup of black coffee in her hands and a boatload of ideas on her mind.

She had awoken before her husband, which was a rare occurrence. He had stayed up late watching a baseball game that went to fourteen innings, so he was still snoozing at almost 8:30 a.m. Colleen and Harvey were both retired, and neither one had anywhere to be on that Wednesday morning, so she let him sleep. *Man, did he yell at that television!* she thought, grinning. Harvey had gotten excited about the game, but his real passion was college basketball. There were nights in early spring when she would hear him cheering "Tar Heels!" in his sleep.

On quiet mornings, when no one else was around, Colleen's mind was especially active. Sitting in the dark, empty kitchen, her thoughts tumbled like a runaway raft on a roaring river, then became ping-pong balls in her brain.

If Harvey were awake, he would be recapping the game for her, even though she had watched most of it with him. The kids hadn't lived at home in over five years. Today wasn't the day she kept her granddaughter. The television and radio were off. Even the songbirds in the backyard were quiet, so Colleen's brain had no distractions to keep it from going into hyper-drive with *what-ifs, maybes,* and *hows.*

The *what-if* of the moment was, *What if I could get on that game show with the good-looking host who asks trivia questions?* And the *maybe* and *how* of the moment was, *Maybe I should go online and find out how to apply to be on the show.*

On any given day, at any given time, Colleen was thinking numerous, similar grandiose thoughts. It wasn't only in the quiet.

She had always been an ambitious woman, perhaps even a little restless. Now that her career was over, Colleen was motivated to find something—something that made her feel like more than just another retiree in suburban Springville, North Carolina. She had more desire now to learn, to see, and to do than she had ever had in her life; and she was always coming up with ideas of things to learn about, places to visit, or ways to make use of her hands and mind.

A couple months earlier, she started trying to memorize the entire book of John in the Bible. *Wouldn't that be impressive!* she had thought. She made it only to the fifteenth verse of the first chapter, but she was still fairly pleased with her efforts. *Maybe I should pick that back up again,* she pondered. It seemed more feasible and more beneficial than going on a game show.

But maybe if I make it on the show—she thought, with a big, child-like grin on her face—*I could win enough money to buy that motorhome Harvey and I have always talked about, and then we could spend more time in the mountains in the fall, when the colors of the leaves just take your breath away! And we can spend more time at the Outer Banks in the spring, when the weather is already hot, but it's still too early for so many vacationers.*

Colleen sat up a little taller in the straight-backed chair, her eyes fixed ahead and widening as she bounced from coast to coast on imaginary travels with imaginary prize money.

She thought it would be nice to see the Grand Canyon or Yosemite, too, but she would never want to stay outside of her home state for long. She was a Carolina girl through and through and had always felt a deep sense of gratitude that she lived in a place where she could be at the mountains within an hour and at the beach within four, with so many pretty places and good people packaged in-between. She even lived in a "Carolina Blue" house, although that wasn't specifically the reason they bought it.

The color of the house was a happy coincidence, but they bought their home because it seemed like the perfect place to raise a family—a quaint house on a quiet street in their hometown.

Colleen took another long sip from a coffee mug she had used for over twenty years. It was white with *World's Best Mom* on it in large, black letters. Coffee was another of the many things for which she was truly and sincerely grateful. Coffee, a good book, perfect four-part harmony, the sight of the first crocuses in spring—Colleen had an aptitude for recognizing simple joys. And despite her longings, it could never be said that she wasn't satisfied with what she'd been given or wasn't grateful for everything she had.

Married to her best friend for thirty-five years, Colleen had a comfortable home and two grown children, whom she saw on a regular basis. She had a beautiful grandbaby, several dear friends, and a loving church family. Her brother and several cousins lived only a thirty-minute drive away. She was in relatively good health, with only a little high blood pressure to mention. She was talented at many things, namely cooking. And she recognized all of these things as gifts from above. That was truly the secret to Colleen's cheerful disposition and pleasant personality.

Still, for a long time, she had harbored a constant, overwhelming sense that there was something she wanted or needed to do that she hadn't yet discovered. The passion she felt for finding and fulfilling an unknown purpose was almost exhausting.

To those that knew her best, the dichotomy of Colleen's life was more than obvious. She was grateful, yet discontent. She was stable, yet wandering. She was liberal, yet conservative. She was liberal with sprays of perfume, affection, and pinches of salt, but not politics; conservative in her theology and with family secrets, but not with kind words or her time.

Harvey was a patient man, and he loved her more than his own life. He not only supported her, but also encouraged almost all the new ideas that her brain continuously churned out. On the rare occasion that he couldn't find it within himself to encourage her, he just stayed quiet until the fire went out on its own. From goat farmer to opera singer, Colleen had considered just about everything in her quest to find an *interesting* path. She hadn't quite risen to the title of *Town Eccentric*, but Harvey, because he loved her, sometimes worried she was on her way.

As Colleen continued to plot and plan, she drummed her fingers on the kitchen table and gazed out her window at a beautiful dogwood tree in full bloom. She learned from her grandmother that Native Americans used the roots of the flowering dogwood to reduce fevers. She wasn't sure if she loved the tree in her yard more for its beauty, its inherent usefulness, or because it reminded her of her grandmother and the wonderful stories she heard sitting on the back porch of the old home place. *Maybe I could study trees*, she thought, her tall forehead crinkling into ridges like planting rows. *I could even join the Arbor Day Foundation! That might be interesting!*

She pressed her forearms into the table as she gripped the cup, making the table creak.

It was partly Colleen's gratitude for the wonders of life—like trees that could be used as medicine—that kept driving her to always find something else to do. She felt that since God made so many beautiful and amazing creations, it was almost irreverent to not take the time to admire and study as much of them as possible. And since God had given her a sturdy mind, it seemed wasteful to not apply it to expanding her knowledge in some way. And since God had blessed her with good health, she believed she should show gratitude by staying active and experiencing life with vigor. At least, that's how she felt now, at this point in life, where she was finally able to pause and look at her circumstances through a different lens.

It seemed every decade or so of her adult life, up to that point, had given Colleen a new set of interests and responsibilities. In her twenties, it was figuring out how to take care of herself, getting a job, getting married, buying a house, and making a home. Her thirties were primarily devoted to keeping two small humans alive and happy and to pouring as much love into their little hearts as she could—all while working to help support the family, to maintain a strong bond with her husband, and to keep the house respectably in order. In her forties, it was a new career as director of the nursing home in Springville and, eventually, the challenges of raising teenagers, which consumed her attention. Her fifties brought fun changes and difficult ones. She cared for her aging parents until their deaths, but she also welcomed her first grandchild.

And there was also the cookbook. Colleen still received lots of attention in Springville for publishing a book that had sold all over the world, thanks to the power of the internet. But she wondered what God had in store for her now. She tried to imagine what would be the hallmark of her current season in life. There were so many exciting and interesting possibilities.

Colleen's brain finally started to wind down from its whirring, and her posture relaxed, as the last of her first cup of coffee was finished. Harvey shuffled into the kitchen in his bedroom slippers just in time to pour her second cup for her; then he joined his wife at the table with a bowl of corn flakes. His eyes were tired, and the lines around them were deep.

Colleen looked at her husband and smiled. Seldom did he come to the breakfast table without dressing for the day first, but she found him handsome in his blue pinstripe pajamas. He owned three identical sets of the collared night shirt with buttons and matching elastic-waist pants. His tousled, dark gray hair was still full and thick, with just a touch of wave.

Before he opened his mouth to speak, Colleen knew what the first topic of the morning would be.

"I still can't get over that game last night. Can you?" Harvey said.

Chapter Two

THE LML

EVERY THURSDAY MORNING AT TEN o'clock, the fellowship hall of Springville Community Christian Church was the meeting place for a dedicated group of women who called themselves the Ladies' Ministry League. The LML consisted of mostly older ladies, and some not-quite-so-old-yet ladies, of the church and a few from other churches in town, whose simple purpose was to find needs and meet them.

Coming together faithfully, the women discussed completed projects, planned new ones, and simply delighted in their fellowship with one another. Fellowship among church ladies was a southern sacrament in itself.

Colleen enjoyed her time with the LML of SCCC for many reasons. It was often one of the best hours of the week for her because it gave her overactive, spinning brain some focus and an opportunity to forge ideas about helping others, instead of about what she could or should do to improve herself or make her life more interesting.

She also enjoyed the company. Since retiring, Colleen missed her coworkers and the patients at the nursing home. She was used to being around lots of people all the time, so the social aspect of the LML was a bonus, added to the purpose of charitable work.

Many of the women that met there had been part of her church family since she was ten years old, and they were some of her favorite people. She felt at home in their presence. It was familiar and comfortable—like a warm blanket on a chilly day.

Nostalgia was one of Colleen's favorite emotions, and there was nowhere else where she felt it more than at the gray, clapboard-sided church building and its adjoining fellowship hall.

They always conducted the meetings in a very business-like manner. But before and after, Colleen enjoyed catching up on whose grandchildren were getting married, who had family moving back to town, who had started taking water aerobics at the big recreation center in the next county, who had tried the new seven-day diet, and who had found the trick to getting rid of those pesky summertime ants.

The fellowship hall was a bright, open space for the meeting. The tables were pushed to the walls on either side of the rectangular room, and the chairs were arranged in a large circle in the center. The back wall of the hall was covered with mirrors, and a table of food was set up on the opposite side of the room nearest the kitchen. Several ladies hovered around the refreshments, agonizing over the always-difficult decision: which of the plentiful appetizers and sweets were most deserving of real estate on the small party plates.

As she sat waiting for the meeting to start, Colleen caught a glimpse of her reflection in the mirrored wall. She studied herself and smiled, thinking how liberating it was to at last be happy with her appearance. At sixty, Colleen was also a little sad that it had taken her so long to get there. She had spent too much of her life being discontent about the size of her hips, wondering if she wore too much or not enough makeup, and worrying about keeping up with that drugstore box color to prevent the grays from peeking through.

She admired herself in the mirror, realizing that she was holding up well. Colleen's confidence was pretty on her. She had wrinkles, but she wasn't ashamed of them. She still never left the house without at least a touch of lipstick and mascara, but she no longer cared if someone thought it was too much. Her backside had done some expanding in an east-to-west manner over the years; but instead of lamenting about it, she chose to be grateful that the metal folding chairs in the fellowship hall were more comfortable than they used to be. She was okay with the little extra padding she carried, as she felt that it made her a more huggable grandma. Most of Colleen's hair still held on to the light blonde hue of her youth, with only a few sections in the front having been taken over by colorless invaders. She no longer tried to camouflage them, and it felt good. At this stage, she finally believed that she was "fearfully and wonderfully made."[1] *I just don't know why I couldn't see that before,* she thought.

Mrs. Whitefield's voice rang out over the din of church lady chatter, calling the meeting to order. The ladies that were still standing settled into their seats—like children hearing the school bell—most with legs crossed at the ankles and plates perched perfectly on knees. They formally started the meeting with a prayer, as was the custom.

The large circle of friends, ready to get to business, consisted of women whose ages spanned a range of over fifty years. They had different skin tones, hair styles, and manners of dress. Some were childless, and some had mothered many more children than had come from their wombs. Some were wealthy, while some knew the challenges of living on a tight budget and too many nights in a row of ramen noodle dinners. Some had grown up on a church pew, and others had

---

1 Psalm 139:14

wandered outside the fold for a long time before hearing the voice of the Shepherd. But they were family, and they had a common mission every time they met—to use their talents and time to represent well the Father they shared.

The ladies collectively performed three separate acts of outreach every week: a service for someone among their group, a service for someone in their church family, and a service for someone or some group in the community. The pastor's wife, Mrs. Marsha Whitefield, who was also chairwoman of the group, implemented the ministry format. While ambitious, it had been a successful approach for many years.

"Good morning, ladies. I trust you've had a blessed week," Marsha said, her face beaming. That was the way she started every meeting. The predictability was another thing that made Colleen's Thursday morning routine so comfortable.

"We'll start by letting the leader of each of last week's projects give their update."

Janice Edwards stood up to report on the ministry effort within the group. One of their members had been caring for her ailing mother, day in and day out for several weeks, so the women organized to provide meals.

There was an understanding in most circles such as theirs: A home-cooked, southern meal was a fitting benefaction in almost all situations—birth, sickness, anniversary, divorce, death. They delivered dinner to their worked-ragged friend on Monday, Wednesday, and Friday of the week prior. More than chicken casserole, beef stew, and meatloaf, the meals represented to their grateful recipient that she was loved and that she wasn't alone.

Another member of the group, a stout woman in her early fifties with a shiny nose and big, bright teeth stood to announce that the church project was complete. She and three other of the LML ladies had spent an entire day scrubbing floors and baseboards in the Sunday school area after days of heavy rain had caused flooding and then mold.

Lastly, Marsha stood up again to give a report. The preacher's wife was a born leader. A petite woman with a big personality, she was direct and knew how to delegate, but she wasn't overbearing. She took the ministry of the LML very seriously because she had a heart for others. Marsha had overseen the community outreach project for the week, and, with great excitement, she reported that they had delivered a total of 592 cans of food to the food bank. Everyone clapped for one another and for their successes. Colleen herself had donated twenty-five cans of soup she picked up on sale at Food Lion.

The food drive was an impressive accomplishment, but the women always reveled in the joy of helping others, no matter the size of the gesture. The unwritten motto of the LML was, "Even if you can only do something small, at least do something."

Colleen couldn't help but think about how most of the ladies there had spent years and years serving their husbands and children by cleaning for them and feeding them. That had been a ministry of its own kind, and now their work for the Lord continued in much the same way.

Any member could submit a ministry idea for consideration, and sometimes there was a backlog of needs. Each week, after selecting the projects, the group assigned members to lead each of the three efforts based on a rotating schedule. It was Colleen's turn to take on a project, so she paid close attention as the group discussed ideas.

Barbara S. suggested they send cards to one of the ladies from LML who was battling an odd case of summer time flu. Barbara B., who was the director of the upcoming Vacation Bible School, recommended the group help her collect and organize craft materials. There were two Barbaras in the group, so the LML, and most of the church, always identified them by their last initial.

Colleen began to think she would be charged with an easy project this go-round. But, as it turned out, cards and crafts were not the tasks to which Colleen was assigned.

"I have a special project I'd like the group to consider," Marsha said, her voice tender, yet authoritative.

"Now, this will be a big commitment, so we need to really consider that." She looked around the circle, trying to read the ladies' faces.

"We haven't tried a project quite like this before, but I am convinced that with God's help, this could be an important ministry that would really make a difference in someone's life!"

Marsha's uncharacteristic hem-hawing made all the ladies a little nervous.

"As a lot of you know," she continued, "I have a cousin that works as director of Oak Grove Children's Home. She called this week to tell me about a situation there." The way Marsha said *situation* got everyone's attention.

"One of the older children at the home has found herself in some trouble." She paused and cleared her throat, as if she wanted to say more but shouldn't.

"Becky—that's my cousin—and the board of directors for the home, have decided the girl needs to be disciplined and that the best way to do that is to have her perform some kind of community service. The goal is to teach her to think about others. Becky hopes we can help the young lady with her community service project as our own outreach project for the community."

Some of the ladies had smiles, and some had looks of concern; but they all nodded in affirmation. As Colleen nodded in agreement, the look on her face was mostly of excitement.

Everyone was very familiar with the children's home. The church took up a collection for them each month and sent gifts over at Christmas. Many of the ladies had dropped off clothes and school supplies in the past, and a handful of the women volunteered on occasion as tutors or to give the houseparents a short break. Colleen had even spent time there reading to the younger children.

"I'm glad you seem excited about this," Marsha said.

The ladies were always anxious to help, but Marsha worried that she was asking a lot this time. She was relieved that no one presented an objection.

"This project will take more than a week, so should we handle multiple projects at a time, or do we want to make this our sole outreach to the community for a while?" Marsha didn't wait for anyone to respond. "For now," she said, "we need someone to organize this effort and get us started."

Colleen liked the ideas of mailing cards and gathering craft supplies, but she had known as soon as the pastor's wife said *special project,* that this was a job she needed to do. For all her wondering and wandering, chasing a thousand little projects in search of fulfillment, there were other times when Colleen knew, without a doubt, what direction to take. At that moment, she was supposed to say yes, and that's what she did.

When Marsha called her name, Colleen chimed, "I'll be happy to help," although she really had no clue what she was getting herself into.

Chapter Three
GRACE

GRACE MARIE HAUSER SAT IN the director's office with a faraway look in her eye and a hidden hurt in her heart.

She hadn't meant to mess up again. "It just sorta happened," she had told one of the houseparents. She didn't have a genuine answer, and that was the best she could do. This time around, the powers-that-be felt they had no choice but to issue a much harsher punishment than normal.

Losing television privileges and computer time and having extra chores were things Grace was used to, but the idea of *community service* made her feel like a criminal. Forty hours of service meant five hours per week for eight . . . whole . . . weeks. *I may be stupid, but at least I know some math,* she thought.

The girl's posture indicated she couldn't care less about what was going on there. She sat with a leg thrown over one arm of the chair, her elbow resting on the other arm as she propped her head up with her hand. There was no remorse for her misdeed. Grace didn't even understand why she should be punished.

Will she ever get off the phone? Grace thought, rolling her eyes with such over-dramatic flair, she hurt herself. She had been sitting in the same uncomfortable chair in that small, stuffy office for over thirty minutes, while the lady rambled on and on about her "options" for service projects. *Since when do I have options?* she thought. *Nobody ever asked me if I wanted to live here. Nobody asked if I wanted to change schools five times in the last three years.*

Grace was getting mad—not at Mrs. Johnson, but at herself. She had resolved a long time ago to never feel sorry for herself. She thought that to show any emotion, to *have* any emotion, was a sign of weakness. And that's one thing she could never afford to be—*weak*.

Suck it up, dummy, her brain told her. *Just do what you have to for four more years. Then you can bust out of this system, and no one will ever tell you what to do again. You'll really have some options then.*

"Okay," Mrs. Johnson said to Grace as she hung up the phone. She took a deep breath, as if to prepare herself for the conversation.

Grace didn't move. She didn't even bother looking at Mrs. Johnson while she delivered her fate.

"You've got a pretty easy gig lined up, young lady." Mrs. Johnson spoke with manufactured sternness. "And I hope you appreciate the strings I was able to pull for you. At the end of the day, my reputation is on the line here, so I sincerely hope you'll pull up your boot straps and get serious about this."

Grace couldn't stand it. "Wow!" she exploded. "Could you fit any more stupid clichés in that speech? Seriously!" She really wished Mrs. Johnson would quit the chit-chat and get to the point.

Becky Smith Johnson was an extremely patient person, and she was very gracious; but her jaw tightened at Grace's disrespect. After a couple of slow, deep, steadying breaths, Becky was calmer. She really did want to help the girl. She wanted desperately to help all fifty of the children at Oak Grove, but she felt drawn to Grace in a special way.

She looked at the teenager sitting across the desk from her and thought, *If only you knew, little girl. If only you knew how valuable you are.*

It would do no good for Becky to *tell* Grace she was valuable. Words meant very little to someone who had been lied to so many times, someone who felt tossed away like three-day-old Chinese takeout. Becky had been praying for a long time that God would send someone into Grace's life who would *show* her.

Becky wore an expression of sympathy as she studied Grace, who had finally looked back at her. The look on Becky's face made Grace even more irritated.

Becky couldn't help but feel sorry for her, but she also admired her, despite the bad attitude. The girl had striking features—sable hair; dark, piercing eyes; and a pretty complexion. It was obvious that Grace was a smart girl, too, and had a sharp wit. But mostly, Becky admired her spirit. She was tough.

It was obvious that Grace's toughness had manifested as disrespect and bad behavior. That's why she was a frequent guest in Becky's office. But that same fortitude was a benefit. Her toughness helped her survive mentally. Her strong will rallied against the circumstances to which she had been subjected.

"I've arranged for you to work with a ladies' group at a local church," Becky said. "They do a lot of community service projects, as well as service within the church, so whatever they assign you to do will count toward your sentence." Becky gave a honey-sweet smile, trying to joke with Grace about her punishment to lighten the mood.

Sentence . . . Grace thought. *Such a strange word. It means "words put together to express a thought" and "a punishment." It can be a noun and a verb.* "*We sentence you to writing sentences for using too many sentences in your sentence.*"

Grace was a deep thinker, although she often played dumb. She had taught herself not to show any positive emotions, like self-worth or a love for learning. Her mind regularly wandered off into deep thoughts while people were speaking to her, especially teachers. It was how she avoided engaging with people and risking them getting too close.

Grace did have a handful of friends at Oak Grove, but only other children. She had written off all adults as untrustworthy a long time ago.

She snapped out of her contemplation as Mrs. Johnson finished with, "You can start next week. I'll go with you to meet some of the ladies, and they will take care of you."

"Nobody takes care of me, but me," was all Grace could manage to mutter, and she left the office without warning, slamming the door behind her.

"You're welcome," Becky offered to an empty room. She decided not to go after the girl.

Feeling discouraged, Becky bowed her head and prayed once again that God would use Grace's mistakes to bring a positive change in her life.

A gentle breeze came in through the open window of the office, bringing a welcome relief to the stifling heat. Becky wondered if it was a sign.

"I know You have something good in store for her, Lord. I just know it."

Chapter Four
PRAIRIE

FRIDAY WAS COLLEEN'S FAVORITE DAY of the week. It was the day she kept her fifteen-month-old granddaughter. Her first and, so far, only grandchild was the reason Colleen had retired early. The childcare arrangements, however, hadn't worked out as planned.

When Colleen's son, Michael, and his wife, Kimberly, found out they were expecting, Colleen was thrilled for the chance to keep the baby while Kimberly worked. But as soon as Colleen made plans to retire, Kimberly's job situation changed.

Although Colleen tried to stay current with trends and the latest technology, she didn't know what telecommuting was before then. It seemed too good to be true that Kimberly could stay at home with the baby and earn an income at the same time. So far, it had worked out okay. But Colleen worried about how stressful it was for Kim. Having a little one around all day meant it took twice as long to accomplish normal work tasks, so her computer was always on well into the evening.

As for Colleen, once they announced her retirement and were already looking for her replacement, she didn't see how she could tell her boss, "Never mind." Her co-workers had already started planning a party, and it just felt like bad manners to mess it up. So, she had stuck with her part of the agreement.

She didn't regret the decision, and she didn't resent her son and daughter-in-law for backing out of the arrangement. All Colleen wanted was the best for her children and grandchild, and it felt like the right time to retire, anyway. She believed everything happened for a reason.

She was thankful that Harvey's retirement account was doing well, and she still received a little income from cookbook sales. They would make it just fine until she was eligible for social security in a couple of years. If there was one thing Colleen believed firmly, proven over and over in her life, it was that the Lord provides.

On Fridays, Colleen and Harvey were the happiest. It was Kim's day to tie up projects for the week; and occasionally, she had to go in to the office for face-to-face meetings, so the doting grandparents had the joy of keeping the sweet little girl all day. In their eyes, the bald, chubby-cheeked, babbling bundle of joy was as close to perfect as a human child could get, with one small exception: her name.

Being someone who admired a good, strong name, it had almost killed Colleen when she first learned her granddaughter would be named *Prairie*. After the baby's parents announced the name, prior to the birth, she had called her best friend, Sherrill, and busted out crying over the telephone. She knew Harvey would laugh at how much she was carrying on about it, but Sherrill seemed to understand her pain—although her own granddaughter's name was Sarah, which means *princess* in Hebrew and was the mother of Isaac in the Bible. Colleen's granddaughter would be called *a tract of grassland*.

"If they like geographical names, why not *Savannah*?" she had wailed to Sherrill. "At least that's the name of a fine southern city. For the love of Pete! Even *Meadow* would have been better!"

Her friend had tried to comfort her by suggesting that Michael and Kim might decide to call the child by the beautiful middle name they had chosen—*Catherine*. But that had sent Colleen into another tizzy because they were spelling it with a *C* instead of using a *K,* which would avoid the child having the same initials as Publisher's Clearing House.

Names, and even initials, were of upmost importance to Colleen.

Whenever she thought about it now, Colleen was embarrassed and ashamed at how she had acted. She had refused to have any baby gifts personalized. She had felt sick to her stomach every time she imagined calling for the girl, in front of all the other grandmothers of Hannahs and Abigails, when it was time to leave the playground. But it finally occurred to her that a unique name would set Prairie apart. It would be an interesting and memorable thing about her. And Colleen appreciated *interesting,* so she had calmed down about it and moved on with life. Still, both grandparents referred to the child as *Sweetie Pie* or *Our Girl* more often than her actual name.

"Is our girl here yet, Collie?" Harvey called from the kitchen. He was the only person in the world allowed to call her *Collie,* especially since she was such a proper name nut. He always told people it was his pet name for her, and he always busted out with a big, booming, throw-your-head-back laugh after he said it. She had heard that joke since she was fifteen years old, and she and Harvey had started dating.

Just then, the doorbell rang, and Colleen went to answer it. On a regular day, Michael would have let himself in. Today, his arms were too full to open the door.

The handsome young man stood there in his business suit, holding Prairie on his hip with one arm and burdened with the latest contraption in baby gear on the other arm. He was quite a sight, juggling the load.

The new activity center Michael delivered was a baby seat with all the bells and whistles to keep the child entertained. Prairie was walking now, and her grandparents needed to be able to contain her for a few minutes at a time and keep her busy.

"There's my sweet baby!" Colleen said, snatching Prairie from Michael's arms. "Oh, I've missed you!"

She promptly began smothering Prairie's chubby cheeks and the top of her head with kisses as she turned and walked to the living room. Michael followed behind with a grin on his face.

"I've missed you, too, Mother," he said.

"Oh, Michael!" Colleen said with a huff. "You know you're still my baby, too!"

Michael was even more handsome with a mischievous grin. He had inherited that trait from his father. After a brief visit with his parents and a good-bye kiss for his daughter, Michael headed off to work, leaving the two grandparents to dote on the child.

Days with Prairie always seemed to fly by; the three of them stayed so busy. Harvey normally took the morning shift with the baby, while Colleen cleaned up the breakfast dishes and did laundry. She loved listening to them play while she worked around the house.

Harvey read books and played pat-a-cake. He sang "Mary Had a Little Lamb" and flew Prairie around the room like a rocket ship. He even gave her a speech about the fundamentals of basketball while they cuddled on the sofa.

He was a wonderful father to their own children, and it surprised Colleen that seeing Harvey as the terrific grandfather that he was seemed to amplify her already-enormous love for him.

Soon, it was time for Colleen to make lunch for Prairie. The two of them were ready for some quality girl time, while Harvey went to work in the garage. The baby watched with curiosity as her grandmother showed her how she put the rice on to boil and how she sliced bananas. Although it would be a while, Colleen looked forward to the day when Prairie would be old enough to cook alongside her.

After lunch, Colleen sat Prairie in the new activity center in the living room and had a captive audience for the big announcement. She hadn't shared her idea with anyone else yet, and she knew Prairie could keep a secret.

Colleen felt that talking to a child just like an adult helped to make them smarter. When Michael and Melody were babies, she had carried on one-sided conversations with them all the time. Now, they were very well-spoken adults, in part, because of their mother's efforts.

"Okay, baby girl," Colleen said. "I'm going to tell you Grammy's exciting news. Poppi doesn't even know it yet!" Prairie giggled as if she knew she was in on something. "I'm going to be on a game show! Well, at least I'm going to try. I have to apply for an audition first, but I have a good feeling about this, sweet girl. The auditions are next month in Raleigh, and I'm going to send in my application! Wouldn't that be something to see Grammy on a game show?"

Prairie had become distracted with the black and white spinning wheel on her activity center, but Colleen continued as if the child was listening and could understand.

"You know Grammy can't stay still. I'm going to do something exciting! Something that will make people say, 'That Colleen Hill—isn't she an interesting lady?'"

Her voice trailed off, and her tone changed, carrying a hint of solemnness. "I just have to find a way to keep things interesting."

Colleen kept talking, until she noticed that Prairie was getting sleepy. She picked her up and sat down in the wooden rocker in front of the picture window. Within a few minutes, the warmth of her grandmother's arms and the gentle motion of the rocker had lulled the baby into a peaceful sleep, and the sweet sound of Prairie's soft breaths, for a few blissful moments, blocked out the competing action in Colleen's brain.

The nap was quick, and Prairie was soon ready to play again, now with a renewed energy. Colleen and Prairie played chase around and around the living room sofa. Colleen sang a hymn for Prairie, then her favorite song by The Beatles as she danced her around the room. They snuck up on Poppi, and he pretended to be scared. They had a snack of strawberries and yogurt. And they relaxed and snuggled while watching the baby channel on television for a few minutes.

Colleen and Harvey were both in love with the child, and their time with her was worth more than gold to them. Caring for Prairie reminded them of their early days as parents. She had dimples, just like her daddy had when he was a baby, and her calm nature reminded them so much of Melody. Just when it seemed that raising children was over, they got to experience its joy again with Prairie.

After Prairie's mother picked her up late in the afternoon, Colleen plopped down next to her husband on the sofa. He reached over and patted her on the knee.

"Whew! Harvey, how did I ever take care of the twins at that age?"

"By the grace of God!" he said smiling. "You were also quite a bit younger back then, baby," he couldn't resist adding. "You were a great mama. You still are. And now you are a great grandma, too. Well, not a great-grandma, but, you know what I mean . . . "

It seemed that at sixty-two, Harvey was just as goofy and mischievous as he was as the twelve-year-old boy who had put rocks in her peanut butter and jelly sandwich at school, although his jokes were much less harmful now. One capped tooth and a gold wedding band hadn't come very far apart, it seemed. Now, here they were, exhausted but happy after another Friday caring for their grandchild.

Chapter Five

MELODY

MELODY ELIZABETH HILL HUNG UP the phone from her mother with a happy heart and a smile on her face. For many years she had been her mother's best confidante, and she had no idea before now that she was being replaced. She laughed out loud when she found out Prairie had become the first to know her mother's secrets.

"Mama," she had said to her pointedly, "why do you want to be on a game show? You already have your claim to fame with the cookbook."

"Oh, this isn't about fame," Colleen told her. "It's about keeping life interesting, you know. Setting goals and seeing if you can accomplish them! It's a challenge!" Colleen's tone suggested confusion as to why Melody didn't naturally fall in line with her thinking.

Melody had goals, too, but they were much different than her mother's. She simply wanted to work, make enough money to support herself, help others when she could, and enjoy life. She found little value in attempting challenges for the sake of being challenged. Her attitude wasn't complacency; it was just a feeling of *enough*. She liked her apartment; it was enough. She had a few good friends; they were enough. She had a good job; it was enough. She was a pretty good person; she was enough.

Her mama, on the other hand, was always striving for more knowledge, more talents, more projects, and more of anything to help validate her existence. When her mother told her about the project she would soon be starting with the LML, about the troubled girl and her required service, Melody worried that she was stretching herself too thin this time.

"Mama, you know I'm proud of you, and it's so great to help, but when are you going to slow down and enjoy retirement?" she had asked her. "Why do you want to take on another project?"

The explanation she received was the same one Melody had heard in the past, on other occasions when her mother seemed driven by inexplicable desire. "I just feel like I need to."

The rest of their phone conversation was about things like Melody's new boss and other changes at the pharmaceutical company where she worked, her friend Macy's wedding plans for the fall, and about Colleen's recent visit to see Uncle Bill. It always made Melody happy to talk with her mama, and she was thankful they were so close. So many of her friends complained about their mothers, but Melody had never shared in their bitterness. For as long as she could remember, she and her mother had been best friends.

Melody plopped down on the couch, folding her legs underneath her. The quiet apartment was peaceful and cozy. Sparsely furnished, it had everything she needed and nothing more. A single lamp lit the entire space, creating a soft glow.

She turned on the television. There it was, the game show about which her mom was so excited—*Risk and Reward with Rodney Vaughn*. She laughed out loud as she imagined her mother on the stage with two other contestants, racing to answer trivia questions as a team before time ran out, and wagering part of their winnings from each round to move on to the next.

Her mother was a sharp lady. Melody thought Colleen might do very well on a show like that. But she also thought that with the number of applicants there must be for the regional auditions, the odds of getting to the show were not in her mother's favor.

"I guess the possibility is kind of exciting, though," she said aloud to no one. "Things work out like they're supposed to."

One thing Melody did share with her mother was faith.

Everything about Melody was average, except for the level of her faith and the level of her contentment. Those had always been above-average.

She wasn't unattractive, but she wasn't the homecoming queen. She hadn't graduated at the top of her class, but she wasn't unintelligent. She was somewhere in between outgoing and shy. She was of medium-height and medium-build and had medium-length hair. And she had a deep, settled peace that she was exactly as she was supposed to be.

Melody left the television on after the game show. She was happy to be spending her evening mindlessly viewing whatever came on. That was how she spent most evenings.

The next program was a reality show about a family with lots of kids. She laughed, thinking the parents resembled the little old lady who lived in a shoe.

The show was entertaining enough. It also reminded her how satisfied she was that she had no one to take care of but herself. She could come and go as she pleased. She spent her money how she wanted. She wasn't accountable to anyone, except God. And she was happy.

Maybe someday, she thought. *But for now, I'm content.*

Chapter Six

THE PLAN

"I'M TELLING YOU, HARVEY . . . my only plan for this weekend is to submit that application . . . and to go to church, of course," Colleen said during breakfast. She had revealed her game show plans to him on the way to the diner, and she sounded determined to make them a reality.

It was a Saturday morning tradition for the two of them to have breakfast at Cecil's Speedy Diner. The diner was only about a five-minute drive from their house in the middle of town, and every once-in-a-while, on days when they felt ambitious, they walked there.

The diner was the same greasy spoon found in most small towns, except it was theirs. Harvey always got the steak and eggs with toast, and Colleen always got biscuits and gravy with a side of grits and heartburn.

Harvey smiled at his bride from across the table. She knew that smile well. It was the smile that meant, *I think you're crazy, but I love you; so, do whatever you want to do, and I'll support you.*

Lots of familiar faces filled the diner as usual. Because Springville was a small town, the people with whom Colleen and Harvey had breakfast at the diner were lots of the same people with whom they went to church, and the grocery store, and the movies, and the car wash, and Walmart. It wasn't uncommon for them to eat their grits and eggs cold, since it was bad manners not to drop your fork when a neighbor stopped by the table to say hello. Between the unplanned but pleasant visits with the other patrons, Colleen and Harvey enjoyed their food and discussed Colleen's newest pursuit.

"The deadline is Monday, and I'm so glad I made up my mind to do this before it's too late. As soon as we get home, I'm going to go online and start entering the application. I've looked at it already. They want so much information! It might take me hours," Colleen said, gesturing excitedly with her fork, then scooping up grits with her toast.

Harvey thought Colleen was even prettier when she was fired up about a new idea. She was so full of excitement and life that she seemed to glow.

"I'm telling you, Harvey, I have a really good feeling about this."

Harvey continued to smile and nod. He was a man of few words, except when it came to sports, but that was a great complement to Colleen's propensity for verbalization. She had always been quite the talker.

A waitress in blue jeans, a t-shirt, and an apron, came to refill Colleen's coffee cup. She hadn't worked there long and didn't wear a name tag, but Colleen recognized her as a classmate of Melody and Michael's. "How are you today, sweetie?" she asked.

The simple question brought light to the young woman's tired eyes. "Just fine, Mrs. Hill," she responded with a smile. "Are you doing okay today?"

"I'm right as rain," Colleen answered, offering a friendly smile back. She looked the young lady in the eye, and she reached over and patted her on the hand when she spoke to her. That was Colleen's way, an extra effort to show her happiness to be near someone.

"What about your project for the church?" Harvey asked after the waitress left. "Doesn't that start soon?"

"Oh, yeah! I'm excited about that, too," she answered. "I have some ideas about what the girl and I will be doing, but I have to talk to Marsha and the director of the children's home first. The director is supposed to call me Monday morning, and then I'll get to meet the girl Tuesday afternoon."

"That sounds good," her husband said. He reached across the table and squeezed her hand. He leaned forward a bit and searched her eyes before speaking again, making sure she was still in the moment and hadn't moved on to the next thought in her brain. "I'm proud of you, Collie."

The two of them finished up their food and coffees and paid the bill, leaving a generous tip for the waitress. Just like she had planned, Colleen went straight to the computer as soon they got home.

Her home office was a pleasant place to work. It had once been Melody's bedroom. As she sat down at the desk, Colleen had a flashback of a little blonde-haired girl playing with Barbie dolls in the corner, and the vision made her smile.

Slipping on her reading glasses, Colleen shook off the feeling of nostalgia and got to work. *I wish I knew how many people have already applied*, she thought as she made her way to the website for *Risk and Reward with Rodney Vaughn*. But it really didn't matter to her. Colleen's intuition was hardly ever wrong, and she knew that a television appearance was in her future.

She worked hard on the lengthy application, her fingers tapping away with skill at the keys. Most of the entries needed to be in essay format, which wasn't a problem. Colleen enjoyed writing about her hobbies and interests almost as much as she enjoyed talking about them. She had a great sense of satisfaction as she clicked the final *submit* button.

There wasn't time to bask in that feeling, however, because just then, the phone rang.

When Colleen answered, she was surprised to find that the caller was Becky Johnson from Oak Grove Children's Home. "So good to hear from you, Mrs. Johnson," she said. "I didn't think you would be calling until Monday."

"I know," Mrs. Johnson said with unnecessary guilt in her voice. "I'm sorry to be calling on the weekend, but Mondays are my busiest day of the work week, so I'm trying to mark some things off my to-do list today."

Colleen assured her it was fine. She was very happy to discuss the details of the arrangement sooner rather than later.

"I really appreciate your help with this, Mrs. Hill," Mrs. Johnson told her. "Grace really isn't a bad girl. She's just been dealt a bad hand."

Grace. Now there's a good name, Colleen thought. *A really good name.* Just the sound of the word gave Colleen a warm feeling.

"Since you've volunteered with us before, we have all the background information we need on you," Mrs. Johnson continued. "I'll just tell you a little bit about Grace and about our recent situation. I can't give you all the details, of course, but to start, Grace is in trouble because . . . "

Colleen interrupted as politely as she could. "If it's okay, Mrs. Johnson, I'd rather not know why she's in trouble," she said. "I'm afraid it might give me a notion about the child before I've had a chance to meet her."

Colleen's attitude surprised Mrs. Johnson, but she respected it. "All right," she replied. "I think that's an admirable mindset."

Mrs. Johnson went on to tell Colleen a little about Grace's past— about how she came to live at Oak Grove after having lived in two other facilities and several foster homes in different counties. She omitted any information about Grace's family, or lack thereof, and the circumstances which had led to Grace becoming a ward of the state at the age of six.

Naturally, Colleen felt sympathy in her heart for the girl, but Grace's story also intrigued her. Based on the information Mrs. Johnson provided, Grace had lived a very interesting, albeit sad and lonely, life. Colleen had always loved meeting and knowing interesting people, and hearing about Grace made her anxious to meet the girl.

What Colleen considered interesting about a person was different from most people's definition of interesting. People who were especially kind or jolly for no apparent reason and people who had a vast amount of knowledge about common things like birds or plants fascinated Colleen. She found people interesting who had been through difficult circumstances and yet had made something of their life, people who had suffered great heartache and yet still expressed gratitude toward their Maker. In her part of the country, it seemed those kinds of people were a dime a dozen, but, nonetheless, interesting.

"Now, my cousin Marsha told me you will handle organizing the service hours, as well as overseeing them. Maybe you can tell me what you have in mind," Mrs. Johnson said.

As they talked, it thrilled Mrs. Johnson that Colleen had already put together a plan, and it thrilled Colleen that Mrs. Johnson approved of her ideas. She hadn't been exactly sure of the requirements, except that the girl needed to use her time in some way as a benefit to others.

The ladies decided that Grace and Colleen would meet for two-and-a-half hours on Tuesdays and two-and-a-half hours on Wednesdays for the next eight weeks. They would spend Tuesday's time cooking and delivering food to a women's shelter and Wednesday's time doing housework for and visiting with Colleen's friend Mr. Hartman, who was eighty-eight years old and confined to a wheelchair.

"Well, I think we have a plan," Mrs. Johnson said. "Those sound like excellent projects for a young girl to learn how to be helpful to others." Her tone was sincere. "I appreciate this so much. But I'm really surprised you haven't recruited any of the other women to help work with Grace. I'm sure there are several who would love to be involved. Are you sure you want to take on such a big commitment on your own?"

"Well," Colleen replied, "I'm retired, so I need something to do with my time." She let out a little chuckle, then with a more serious tone said, "Besides, I feel like I need to do this."

Chapter Seven

THE MEETING

ON SUNDAY, THE PASTOR OF Springville Community Christian Church preached a powerful message on the verse from Psalms that says, "Be still and know that I am God."[2] For a moment, Colleen thought the pastor might be speaking to her, but she dismissed the idea before rushing home to fix a huge lunch.

Sunday lunch was not a meal. It was an event, with the whole family in attendance. The table setting wasn't fancy, but the food was unmatched; and to everyone there, so was the company. It was the kind of afternoon that made Colleen sigh over and over again with contentment.

The joy of spending time with her family was still fresh in Colleen's heart on Monday morning, and the happy memories that lingered helped propel her into the busy week she had planned. Her first task of the day centered around the cookbook.

Although seven years had passed since the cookbook was first published, it was still available online. Sometimes she received emails and letters from readers. Her favorite so far was from a lady in Denmark who tried her recipe for Southern Shrimp and Grits, but substituted herring for the shrimp. The lady raved about it in her letter, but Colleen wasn't so sure. Still, she appreciated knowing that her little collection of

---

2 Psalm 46:10

recipes had reached so far. Food had a way of bringing people together. Every Monday morning, Colleen went through the correspondence and replied to each of them.

As she worked, she caught herself humming the theme song to *Risk and Reward with Rodney Vaughn*. Becoming aware of her Freudian music-making, Colleen began to hum more loudly, with intention, even throwing in an air guitar solo as the song came to its dramatic conclusion.

She grew more excited by the day waiting to receive an email from the show. *Maybe I'll tell Grace that I'm going to be on a game show,* Colleen thought. *That might give us something to talk about.*

Colleen was excited about her meeting with Grace and Mrs. Johnson, too. When she finished with the "cookbook chores," as Harvey liked to call them, she started preparing for guests. And having guests always meant cooking.

In the kitchen, she busied herself mixing made-from-scratch brownie batter and making a fresh gallon of sweet tea. Colleen added a little extra sugar to the tea, so its sweet taste wouldn't be lost to the tongue, compared to the sweetness of the dessert. While the brownies baked, filling the kitchen with a smell so good it made one want to lick the air, she sat down at the kitchen table to finish the crossword puzzle in the morning paper. She hoped word puzzles would help keep her sharp for her game show appearance.

At 2:00 p.m., the doorbell sounded, and Colleen wasted no time in answering it. She opened the door to see Mrs. Johnson—a slim, neatly dressed lady—standing on the covered front porch, smiling at her.

Mrs. Johnson was in her early forties. Her strawberry hair was styled in a cute bob, and she wore dark-framed eyeglasses, which sat atop a freckled nose. Even before Colleen could open the screen door all the way, Mrs. Johnson had her hand extended for a handshake.

"Come in, come in!" Colleen exclaimed warmly, taking Mrs. Johnson's extended hand in both of her own. "It's so nice to see you, Mrs. Johnson." As she ushered the lady over the front door threshold, she looked out at the porch, expecting her newest project to be standing there. But Mrs. Johnson was alone.

"Please, call me Becky," Mrs. Johnson said.

"Okay, Becky," Colleen said, a bit worried. "But, where's my new friend? Isn't she with you?"

"Oh, Grace is in the car. One of our houseparents is waiting with her. She's feeling a little shy today, plus . . . I want us to talk by ourselves for a moment, anyway." Colleen led Becky to the sofa, where the two ladies sat down.

"Mrs. Hill . . . " Becky began.

"Colleen," Colleen corrected.

"Colleen . . . I just want to tell you again how much we appreciate this. I think meeting some new people will be really good for Grace. It's very important that she learn how to serve others, how to consider other people."

It was obvious that Becky cared about Grace. Her words were so earnest, almost pleading. Colleen sat on the edge of the sofa, letting Becky know she was listening and that she understood.

"Grace has a pretty bad attitude about life right now, and dealing with her requires a lot of patience," Becky said, now with reservation. "What I wanted to tell you, that I didn't say on the phone is, if at any time you feel like the arrangement isn't working out, and you want to stop volunteering with Grace, I'll understand. You are under no obligation. Really."

Becky expected Colleen to ask questions about Grace's behavior or to ask for advice on dealing with her. She expected to see her squirm a little. Instead, Colleen just said, "Okay. I think we'll be fine."

There was paperwork to sign to renew Colleen's volunteer status with the children's home. Harvey had stopped by Becky's office earlier in the day to do the same, since Grace would be spending time in their home. When it was all finished, Becky went to the car to retrieve Grace.

Normally, Colleen would have gone to meet any new guest at the front door, or even the front step, but something inside told her to keep her seat on the sofa and wait for Grace to come in. She thought rushing to greet the child might overwhelm her.

When Becky came back, a sulky, sour-faced girl followed reluctantly behind her and into the living room. She hardly looked fourteen; Grace was small for her age. *Why, you're no bigger than a minute!* Colleen thought about saying, but didn't.

Colleen's eyes followed her. *She looks like such a normal girl,* she thought. She understood that Grace was a normal girl, but the circumstances of her young life had been far from the common definition of the word.

Grace wore denim shorts, a solid black t-shirt, and black flip flops with sequins on the straps. She carried a tiny pocketbook on her right shoulder and an invisible chip on the other. Reaching out to stroke the plush, brown fabric of the sofa as she passed by it, the look on her face was an odd mixture of fascination and disgust. The group home where she lived was comfortable, but somewhat institutional. It wasn't homey like this.

Grace plopped down in the matching armchair across from the sofa, letting herself get absorbed right away into its fluffy cushions. Rather than helping with an introduction, Becky gave Grace and Colleen space to approach each other in their own way.

"Hi there, Grace," Colleen said. "It's so good to meet you. I'm Colleen." Colleen didn't expect a reciprocal greeting, and she didn't make the girl uncomfortable by waiting for one. "Do you like brownies?"

Grace wasn't sure how to answer the question. She adored brownies. *Who doesn't?* she thought. But she wasn't going to fall for the niceties. She realized, however, that she couldn't just sit there without saying anything, so she only said, "Sure."

Colleen left the room and came back soon, carrying a tray with three plates and three glasses. Grace was a little impressed that Colleen had obviously prepared the tray ahead of time.

She set the tray on the coffee table and proceeded to serve her guests. Colleen had used her best plates for the occasion because she wanted to make Grace feel special and welcomed.

She handed Becky a plate with a still-warm brownie, but the plate she handed Grace held two of the yummy treats. Grace tried to hide her pleasure as she took a bite, but it wasn't easy. They were the best brownies she had ever tasted.

Colleen left the glasses of tea on the tray, in reach of all three ladies, and sat down with her own plate of dessert to enjoy.

"Thank you for your hospitality. These are very good!" Becky said. "Would you like to tell Grace about the projects you've decided on? Once she knows all about what she'll be doing, she'll be ready to get to work tomorrow."

As Colleen started talking, Grace surveyed the room, the main living space of the home. She hadn't thought about what to expect of Colleen or her home. She didn't really care. She was just there to put in her time and get out. But she had to admit it was a welcoming place—mostly neat and tidy, but with just enough clutter to put a person at ease.

Grace caught bits and pieces of what Colleen was saying. *Shelter . . . cooking . . . nice ladies . . . veteran . . . wheelchair . . . housecleaning . . . church.* She took a bite of brownie that was too big for her mouth and studied several framed photographs on the mantel while she chewed. A large one in the middle stood out. It wasn't a studio portrait. It was taken in the front yard of the house in which she now sat. She recognized a younger, slimmer Colleen in a yellow Sunday dress and wide-brimmed hat. A broad-shouldered man in a gray suit stood with his arm around her. Two children, the same height, stood in front of the couple, also in their Sunday best, wearing big smiles and holding Easter baskets. She found herself captivated by the image, but she didn't know why. *They all look so happy,* she thought. *I wonder what they're so darn happy about.*

Chapter Eight
THE FIRST DAY

ON THEIR FIRST OFFICIAL DAY of working together, Colleen felt hopeful. It seemed Grace had resigned herself to the idea of being there and doing what she had to do. She was far from warm, or even cordial, but neither was she disrespectful. No eye rolls or big shrugs, just all business, and Colleen thought that was a very good place to start.

Since Grace skillfully eluded all attempts to get to know her, Colleen spent most of the time talking about herself. Her goal was to let Grace get to know her, whether she wanted to or not. And because talking was an art to Colleen, she had no problem rattling on and on while she worked. She just pretended Grace was hanging on to every word.

The job of the day was to make vegetable beef soup for the women's shelter. It was an easy dish to make and an old standard. Colleen liked to think of it as comfort in a bowl.

There weren't a lot of women from Springville who needed to make use of the shelter there, but it was the only one of its kind in the entire county. A worthy ministry, there was always at least a few women and children taking refuge there at any given time.

"Grace, can you dump these tomatoes in the pot?" Colleen asked. "I canned these myself last year." The LML would reimburse Colleen for the cost of groceries for the project, but the homegrown ingredients were her own contribution.

Grace did as she was instructed while Colleen started chopping an onion. "Honey, when you're finished with that, grab the corn out of the freezer, please, and go ahead and add that, too."

In between sniffles from the effects of the onion, Colleen told Grace all about Melody and Michael, about Harvey, and about Prairie. She told her about her first job at the car dealership and then her career at the nursing home.

"It was a wonderful job," Colleen said. "I really felt like I was helping people there." *Sniff, sniff.* "I got to make sure that the residents were taken care of, that their needs were being met." *Sniff.* "I enjoyed being responsible for them, y'know? Those sweet, old folks didn't really have any other option than to be there." *Sniff.*

"I know how they feel," Grace said under her breath, before she realized it.

"What's that, honey?" Colleen asked, surprised that Grace had finally volunteered to speak.

"Nothing."

"Well, I miss my old folks. I call them that with respect, of course. Some of them weren't that much older than me, anyway. But they had so much wisdom to share with me." Colleen gestured with the knife in her hand as she spoke. "And they taught me how good it can feel to help others. I believe, after a couple of weeks of us working together, you're going to learn that, too."

She looked over and realized that Grace had finished with the tomatoes and corn and had already added the ground beef to the pan on the stove without being told. The girl showed a little bit of initiative, and it impressed Colleen, although she kept the thought to herself.

"The ladies are going to enjoy eating this for dinner tonight! And the little ones, too," Colleen said. She put the onions in the pan with the beef. "When you're done with that, you can drain these cans of beans and add them to the pot."

Colleen stood back and watched Grace at work.

"You're doing an excellent job, my friend!" Colleen said.

Grace kept stirring the beef and onions. She thought about saying thank you, but the idea faded quickly. Instead, she said, "I guess so." Coming up with responses that weren't friendly but also wouldn't get her into trouble was becoming difficult.

"You know something?" Colleen said. "I just realized I don't know your last name. What is it?"

"Why does it matter?" Grace asked, not disrespectfully, but with genuine curiosity.

"I just want to get to know you better," Colleen explained. "Plus, I think names are important. Don't you think so?" Colleen chuckled a bit. "The Bible says, 'A good name is rather to be chosen than great riches'![3] Of course, it isn't talking about what's on your birth certificate, though, is it?"

"Uh . . . well . . . it's Hauser," Grace offered. Colleen smiled and nodded. She didn't comment further, but she was happy that Grace hadn't shut her down.

The soup was almost ready, and the kitchen smelled wonderfully of the happy blend of meat and vegetables in the savory tomato base. Colleen had bought some loaves of French bread, and Grace put the finishing touches on the meal by slicing the loaves, then covering the bread in plastic wrap to take to the shelter.

The seasoned chef and the beginner cook finished their preparations and, working together, loaded the results of their labor into Colleen's

---

3 Proverbs 22:1a

SUV. The giant pot of soup was heavier than Grace imagined it would be. It took them both to lift and carry it, and they had to be careful not to let any slosh out as they put it down in the passenger-side floorboard. Grace was to make sure the pot didn't tip while Colleen drove.

Most of the car ride to the shelter was quiet. Colleen felt like she had run her mouth enough for one day, and a little quiet wouldn't hurt. But just before they arrived at the shelter, she remembered she hadn't told Grace about her plan.

"Oh, guess what, honey!" she said. "I'm trying to get on television!"

Grace looked confused. She didn't realize Colleen was cleverly baiting her to engage in conversation. Colleen waited several awkward seconds.

"What do you mean?" Grace finally asked.

"I've submitted an application to be on *Risk and Reward*. I'm just waiting on them to contact me! Do you know the show?"

Grace found the idea of Colleen being on a game show amusing. She could just imagine her on stage, with all the bright lights, telling stories in between each question and calling Rodney Vaughn *honey*.

"Yeah, I've seen it," she said, with a hint of a smile.

"Well, I just can't wait. And once I mark that off my list, I'll find another goal! You gotta keep moving in life, y'know. Gotta keep things interesting!"

Grace found Colleen's exuberance about life annoying, like a fly that keeps landing on your picnic plate.

"I might try zip-lining next. Have you ever thought about it? How amazing would *that* be? I don't think I know many people who've done that."

Colleen put on the turn signal as she approached their destination. It was only a fifteen-minute drive to the shelter in the former fellowship hall of Westside Baptist Church, on the westside of Springville, as the name suggested.

Some months earlier, the church built a bigger space in which to hold events, and they converted the old space into the Westside Center for Women and Children. The ministry seemed so important that church leaders were considering giving the women and children the new building and going back to having their potlucks and wedding receptions in the smaller space.

Colleen and Grace delivered the food to its grateful recipients in time for an early dinner. "Normally, I would let this soup simmer all day long, but it will still be good," Colleen said to Grace as they carried in the soup.

Grace had never been inside a group home that wasn't only for children. She noticed the cots and duffel bags lining the perimeter of the dining hall, and she was confronted with a harsh reality. The women there had very limited options in life right now, too, although they were grown.

On the way back from the car with the sliced bread, Grace noticed a little girl, about four years old, waiting for dinner. The girl, standing and facing her seated mama, looked into eyes which were almost too swollen to look back.

The sight sent Grace to a place in her memory that she had forgotten existed. For a moment, she was the little girl. She suddenly wanted to run to the pair, and she wanted to run away at the same time, run as far and as fast as she could. Instead, she stood frozen. Coming to herself, and not wanting to be caught staring, she made her way to the kitchen, where Colleen was waiting.

Grace was a master of disguise when it came to emotion, so Colleen didn't notice any change. But Grace had felt a change, and she didn't like it.

Chapter Nine

MR. HARTMAN

ROBERT JAMES HARTMAN WAS DELIGHTED to have an extra visitor. It had been a long time since he last saw a child in person. The only visits he ever received were from Colleen, the pastor, and the nice, young nurse from the agency, who came three times a week.

His home was out in the country, on a dead-end dirt road with three other houses, on a small lot. Several apple trees stood around his house, almost in a circle, like sentries guarding a castle. The little house was decades older than Mr. Hartman, but it had been remodeled many times over the years to keep it in good condition. He had lived there with his wife until her death five years earlier. Their only child had passed on before them.

Grace was visibly uncomfortable being at Mr. Hartman's house, and Colleen felt a little bit sorry for her. In the car, she had voiced concern that she wouldn't know what to do or how to act around the old man. Colleen thought it was a good sign. It meant that she actually did care—at least a little. *You're starting to come around*, Colleen thought. She assured Grace that Mr. Hartman was a very nice man and that she would do fine.

Grace was so determined to stay detached, to not feel anything. But something happened when she saw Mr. Hartman in his wheelchair, in his lonely house. Despite her intentions, she couldn't let herself be a jerk to him.

"Hot out there today, isn't it?" Grace asked after Colleen introduced them. She instinctively spoke loudly, in case Mr. Hartman didn't hear well. She had always noticed adults talking about the weather when they didn't know what else to talk about.

"I wouldn't know," Mr. Hartman replied, in a normal volume. "I haven't been outside in the last week. And since I had central air installed a few years back, I can keep it any temperature I want in here. I keep it on seventy-five in the summer, to help keep the electric bill down." His voice was much stronger than his appearance suggested.

Grace didn't know what to say next; but Colleen rescued her, and she was grateful.

"Grace is a new friend of mine," Colleen told Mr. Hartman. "She'll be joining me on my visits with you for the next few weeks. Is that okay with you?"

Colleen hadn't discussed the service project with Mr. Hartman. He was a very agreeable person, and she knew he wouldn't mind a surprise guest.

"Fine with me," Mr. Hartman said, with a wave of his frail hand.

"Since you haven't been outdoors in a while, what do think about some fresh air?" Colleen asked. "You're lookin' a little pale. Some sunlight might do you good." She patted his knee and smiled at him warmly.

"That sounds pretty good to me," he said. "I just can't get this old chair out by myself. Do you want to help me, young lady?" he asked, turning to Grace.

"Um . . . " Grace stammered.

"Go on, honey," Colleen said. "The fresh air will do you good, too. I'll stay inside and take care of some of these dust bunnies."

Grace inched toward Mr. Hartman; then, with a look of concern on her face, she took control of the chair, her fingers fumbling at first to grip the handles the right way. She pushed him, as he directed, through the kitchen and to the back door.

Getting him over the threshold leading to the back deck proved to be a challenge. She attempted it with a little too much force, and the chair bumped, almost tipping Mr. Hartman out. Finally, she succeeded, and he didn't even complain about the bumpy ride. Stepping out onto the deck in the warm sunshine, Grace felt a sense of accomplishment.

"Do you mind pushing me to the other side of the deck?" Mr. Hartman asked. "I want to see my mountains."

"Your mountains?" Grace asked, as she did as he wanted.

"Yeah. From over here you can just make out the tops of part of the Blue Ridge. I've always called them my mountains, but I'll be happy to share them with you." Mr. Hartman winked at Grace.

"Sometimes, after a few days when I can't get outside, I think I hear them calling my name. I've hiked all over those mountains. But that was a long time ago—before my legs gave out on me."

Grace found a deck chair to sit in, facing the yard, while Mr. Hartman soaked up the sunshine and admired the view off to the left. She had to admit, it was a pleasant day, despite the heat. The weather was typical for late June in North Carolina, but the beauty of the bright blue sky, dotted sparsely with wispy clouds, made the heat more bearable.

Grace wore blue jeans, a red tank top, and sandals. She preferred comfort to style, but she was usually able to accomplish both. After a few minutes outside, she wished she had worn shorts.

Mr. Hartman enjoyed having someone to listen to him, about anything and everything. She could see why he and Colleen were friends. They both loved to talk. Grace wondered how many times a day he had a conversation with himself, since, more often than not, there was no one else around.

Grace listened as he talked about the favorite trails he had explored in healthier times. He named several of them and the natural characteristics that set them apart from one another. As he described the landscape, Grace was able to picture in her mind each ridge and bald and every summit and valley.

Mr. Hartman's backyard was peaceful and pleasant. The small rectangle of grass sloped downward just before turning into forest. Grace guessed the slope led to a creek not far beyond the wood line. As she studied her surroundings, she surprised herself by laughing out loud at the sight of a mockingbird dive-bombing a stray cat passing through the yard.

"He must have some babies in a nest close by," said Mr. Hartman. "It's the time of year for 'em." He turned his head to look at Grace. "Did you know those birds can imitate the calls of up to thirty other birds? Ain't that the darnedest thing? They're pretty remarkable creatures." He paused. "And they sure do love my apple trees."

Grace looked out at the pretty yard. The man who lived across the road mowed Mr. Hartman's grass every other week during the summer. It wasn't a favor. He just didn't want his elderly neighbor's unkempt yard to distract from the beauty of his own.

The mockingbird went after the cat again, who appeared to be minding his own business. "It's pretty amazing how that bird defends its young," Mr. Hartman said. "Just a simple animal, and yet smart enough to do what it needs to do to preserve the next generation."

"That bird's a lot better than some people," Grace muttered.

For the better part of thirty minutes, the two had sat there together, until Colleen came to check on them. "You two gettin' along okay out here?" she asked, poking her head out of the back door of the house. "Don't get yourself overheated, Mr. Hartman."

"We're good. She's real good company," Mr. Hartman said, motioning in Grace's direction. "But, it is gittin' a might warm."

Grace recognized the compliment, and it felt nice. She smiled inside, thinking, *Somebody likes my company.*

"I'll take you back inside, Mr. Hartman," Grace said.

Once inside, Grace and Colleen folded the laundry that his aide didn't have time to finish before her last shift ended. After laundry, they found a few more jobs around the house, chatting with Mr. Hartman while they worked.

"You know, with your features, I just bet you've got some Cherokee blood," Mr. Hartman said to Grace, as she straightened magazines on the coffee table.

"Really?" Grace asked, intrigued. "That's kinda cool."

"Has any of your family ever mentioned Cherokee kin?" he asked.

Grace looked down at the floor. "I don't know a whole lot about my family," she said. It was a stock answer she had learned to give in situations such as this. Over the years, her memories of family had gotten fuzzy.

Still being sharp of mind, Mr. Hartman understood not to press. "Well, one of my best army buddies was full-blooded Cherokee," he said. "One of the finest fellers I ever knew. And the history of their people is worth studying, if you haven't learned about it in school. It's a sad past, but one we all should learn from."

"I don't think we've learned about them," Grace said.

"All right then," Mr. Hartman said, "I'm going to give you some homework. The next time you come to see me, I want you to tell me about Sequoyah."

Grace repeated the name slowly to make sure she had heard it correctly. "Okay," she said. "I'll see what I can do."

When it came time to leave, Colleen leaned down and gave Mr. Hartman a goodbye hug. Grace gave a fast, side-to-side wave as she went out the door, and they both wished the man a good rest of the week.

On the way back to Oak Grove, Grace turned to Colleen and seemed to really look at her for the first time. "How do you know him?" she asked.

"Well, let's see," said Colleen, as if she were searching her memory. "We went to church together, back when he was healthy. And he was our mailman for a while, a long time ago. But the nursing home is where I became reacquainted with him." Colleen glanced away from the road to smile at Grace.

"He had a stroke a couple years ago and spent some time with us while he recovered. Truth be told," Colleen said, sighing sadly, "he probably ought to live there now, but the poor fella just can't stand the thought of leaving his home."

If I had a home like that, I wouldn't want to leave it either, Grace thought.

Chapter Ten

THE CALL

THE CALL CAME ON A Friday, not even a week after Colleen submitted her application. She had expected an email, not a phone call, and it caught her off-guard being so soon.

"Mrs. Hill?" the voice on the phone said.

"Yes, this is Colleen Hill." She said it warily, assuming the call was from a telemarketer. Her phone rang about twenty times a day with calls from people trying to sell life insurance or home security systems. She missed the days of people selling *Encyclopedia Britannica* and vacuum cleaners door-to-door. Those people were a lot friendlier and a lot less obtrusive than the nonstop robo calls.

"My name is Amy Nichols, and I work with the Contestant Selection Team for *Risk and Reward with Rodney Vaughn*." The lady's voice was over-the-top cheerful.

"Oh, yes! I'm glad to hear from you." Colleen was excited, but she tried to maintain her calm. She used her phone voice to sound charming, so *you* was a sing-songy two syllables.

"Mrs. Hill, I'm calling to let you know that we've reviewed your application, and we would like to invite you to an in-person audition to be on the show. We think our audience would love you."

"That's wonderful!" Colleen exclaimed.

She rushed to her office for a pen and paper, so she could write down all the details, even though the lady told her she would email them to her. She wanted to make sure she could tell Harvey everything right away.

Miss Nichols told Colleen that the next step in getting on the show was to play a mock version of the game with other potential contestants. The audition would be held on July twenty-first in Raleigh, which was about a two-hour drive from Springville. *That's only a few weeks away!* Colleen thought.

When Colleen hung up the phone, she ran back to the living room, where Prairie was playing in the activity center. "I did it, sweet girl!" she exclaimed. She bent down and planted a big kiss on the baby's forehead. "Grammy's going to be on a game show!"

In her prime, Colleen had been a great dancer. Showing that she hadn't lost her skill, Colleen put on quite a show for Prairie. The baby giggled and bounced as her grandmother danced around her, then around the sofa, around the coffee table, and back around her again. The scene was *Soul Train* meets *America's Funniest Home Videos*.

As the dance party continued, Harvey came through the front door. "They called, Harvey! They called!" Colleen yelled. "I'm on to the next round!"

"Well, that's good," Harvey said, as he scooped Colleen around the waist and led her in a funny jig. "I thought maybe you'd seen a mouse in here."

Prairie watched her grandparents intently. It wasn't the first time she had seen this show. She raised her arms, asking them to pick her up, and they were more than willing to include her in the fun.

As the celebration died down, Colleen handed the baby off to Harvey. "I need to go share the good news," she said, out of breath.

The first person she called was Melody.

"Will you go with me to the audition?" Colleen asked her. "I could use you by my side!"

"You know I will, Mama. I'm super excited for you!"

"It's on a weekday, though. Do you think you can get off work?"

"It will be okay. Work has been really slow lately," Melody replied. There was a tone of concern in her voice.

"Okay. I'm so glad you can go! And, baby, don't worry about your job. Everything will work out. Remember that 'all things work together for good.'"[4]

After talking to Melody, Colleen called Sherrill. That meant that by Sunday, all of Springville Community Christian Church knew about Colleen's exciting news, even though Sherrill didn't attend SCCC.

After the morning service, everyone came up to Colleen, asking questions.

"Are you nervous about the audition?"

"How much money do you think you'll win?"

"When do you get to meet Rodney Vaughn?"

Colleen answered each question much the same way. "It's just an audition. I haven't made it on the show yet." But deep in her heart, she knew it was just a matter of time before she *would* be telling her friends about meeting Rodney Vaughn.

Colleen and Harvey shook hands with the pastor and his wife on their way out, as usual. "I talked to Becky the other day," Marsha said

---

4 Romans 8:28

to Colleen. She sounded excited. "She said she thought your work with Grace Hauser went really well last week! How did you feel about it?"

"To be honest, it was much better than I expected," Colleen answered. "She's quiet, and a little sulky at times, but she did everything I asked her to do. I really enjoyed it."

"That's so good to hear," Marsha said, relieved. "I'm sure she just loved cooking in your kitchen and learning from you. I bet it was a real treat for her." Colleen smiled at the compliment, although she wasn't sure she would have described Grace's experience as enjoyment.

"Remember, you can delegate," said Marsha. "There are several people willing to take over for a week. We can use the fellowship hall kitchen to make meals and deliver them for you. I can take her with me to the nursing home to visit one day. That would be a good opportunity for her, too. All you have to do is tell us you want help."

"I know. And I appreciate it," Colleen replied. "I just feel like this is something I need to do."

"Okay, honey," Marsha said, taking Colleen's hands in hers. "We just don't want you to be stretched too thin."

The thought of over-extending herself was not one that ever plagued Colleen. As she and Harvey made their way across the parking lot of SCCC, another idea bubble burst in her brain and spilled out of her mouth to her husband. That was something he had grown quite used to over the years.

"Oh, Harvey!" Colleen exclaimed. "You know what we should do?" Harvey knew she didn't expect him to answer. "We should start making our own soap. Sherrill's niece owns that lavender farm off the highway, and they just had a big harvest. Oh, how I love the smell of lavender. I bet we could get a bulk discount."

They were almost to the car, and Colleen was no longer talking directly to Harvey, but was still talking. "We could donate it to the shelter. And good soap would make real nice Christmas gifts. Christmas will be here before you know it. Maybe Grace would want to help me make it. Of course, I'd have to learn how, but it can't be hard, can it?"

Harvey drove toward home smiling, not saying a word, listening to his wife's stream-of-consciousness monologue and marveling at her never-ending imagination.

Chapter Eleven

THE COOKBOOK AND TEN DOLLARS

"WELL! YOU CAME BACK!" COLLEEN greeted Grace jokingly on the first day of their second week. On Tuesdays, a houseparent from Oak Grove Children's Home delivered Grace to her door. On Wednesdays, Colleen picked Grace up to go see Mr. Hartman.

"You know I don't have a choice, right?" Grace responded. Colleen thought she detected a hint of humor in her tone.

"Come on in. I've got us all set up in the kitchen," said Colleen. "We're making chicken salad today. It's a special recipe!"

Grace followed Colleen into the kitchen, ready to cook. She hoped things would go as well as they did the week before when they had made soup. Grace washed her hands and started to assess what needed doing first, but a book on the countertop caught her attention.

"Wait a minute!" Grace exclaimed, pointing to the book. "Is that you?"

"Yeah, that's my cookbook," Colleen said, as if everybody in the world had written one, too. Grace ran her fingers over the glossy front cover, staring at Colleen's picture printed right in the center. For the first time, Grace realized that Colleen closely resembled a famous southern chef she had seen on television.

"*Mountain to Sea Cooking* by Colleen C. Hill," Grace read. The book was subtitled "North Carolina Culinary Traditions."

"I was going to call it *Carolina Cooking with Colleen,* but I decided the alliteration sounded a little silly."

All around Colleen's picture on the front of the book were photographs of different parts of the state. There was a picture of a pretty waterfall and an aerial shot of the southern coastline. One picture displayed the silhouette of the unmistakable Pilot Knob at dusk, and another was shot from a dirt path with tall corn growing on both sides. The background of the cover was a pattern of illustrations of different foods.

"Why didn't you tell me you wrote a book?" Grace asked. She sounded almost hurt, like Colleen had withheld an important secret.

"Well, honey, it's just a cookbook. It's not like I'm Fanny Flagg or anything!" Besides the Bible, the only books Colleen had ever enjoyed reading happened to be written by southern women. In addition to Ms. Flagg, Harper Lee and Margaret Mitchell were by far her favorite authors.

Writing a cookbook had been a natural thing for Colleen to do, especially a cookbook that honored her beloved state. She had started cooking at a very young age, and she enjoyed perfecting all the recipes she had accumulated over the years. To Colleen, mixing, measuring, basting, and baking were artforms, and the recipes in her memory were her medium.

"It's a collection of recipes for dishes that are popular in different parts of the state," Colleen explained. "You see, my daddy managed textile mills when I was little, and he got moved around a lot. I've lived in all three regions of this great state—the Mountains, Piedmont, and Coast. Four, if you count the Sandhills separately from the Coastal

Plain. But we settled in Springville when I was ten. My cookbook includes local specialties from all over."

The cookbook wasn't just about food. It was a way to pay homage to the place she was proud to call home, the place that had helped mold her into who she was. Grace didn't even try to hide her interest.

"I also came up with a few recipes that feature products born in North Carolina, like Pepsi-Cola Pound Cake and Texas Pete Tater Soup. The best hot sauce in the world is made just down the road. Did you know that?" Colleen asked.

Grace could tell that Colleen enjoyed talking about her claim to fame and was passionate about cooking and about her home.

"That's pretty cool, I guess," Grace conceded. "What else ya got in here?" she said, pulling her long, loose hair into a ponytail and securing it with the elastic she wore on her wrist.

"Take a look," Colleen said. "I think you'd like the Krispy Kreme Peach Cobbler and the Cheerwine Cupcakes. Oh, I do love sweets! There are a few stories in there, too. Just family anecdotes that go along with some of the recipes. Wait, here," Colleen said, opening a cabinet and retrieving a copy from a tall stack. "You can keep this one."

Grace took the book from Colleen as if it were paper money. She flipped through it, scanning the recipes. There were recipes that called for North Carolina blueberries and sweet potatoes. There was even a recipe for kudzu jelly.

"Well, we better get to cooking," Colleen said. "The chicken salad isn't going to make itself. Oh, and we happen to be using a product made right here in North Carolina—Mt. Olive Pickles."

Colleen let Grace continue flipping through the pages while she started cooking on her own. Sometimes, Grace paused to study one more carefully. It was surprising to Colleen how captivated Grace seemed by the book.

Eventually, Grace joined Colleen in her work, and the pair finished the dish of the day together. They loaded the chicken salad, sandwich rolls, and fresh fruit into the car, and started out for another delivery to the shelter.

Springville had only one major intersection, Spring Street and Market Street. Pulling up to the stoplight there, Colleen and Grace encountered a rare sight for their town. A man with tattered clothes and an unshaven face stood holding a sign. He had a backpack on his back and a scruffy dog laying at his feet. The dog was panting, and the man was without sunglasses or a hat to protect him.

As they approached, Colleen rolled down the window and handed the man a rolled-up bill she had dug out of her purse. She exchanged pleasantries with him, commenting on the brutal weather as casually as if she were talking to the mailman, instead of a vagrant begging for money on the side of the road.

Grace watched the transaction with intense curiosity. When the light changed to green, Colleen gave the man another nod and a smile. "God bless you!" she said.

Colleen had driven less than ten feet past the stoplight when a perplexed Grace burst out, "Why on earth would you do that? That was a ten-dollar bill you just gave away! Are you rich or something?"

"Hardly," Colleen replied, surprised that the interaction had evoked the most consecutive words yet from Grace.

"Well, do you know him? Is he a relative?" Grace persisted.

"In a way, we're all related. But, no, I don't know him."

Grace was still dumbfounded. "Look, I get helping out the old guy. He's your friend. And I think it's pretty cool taking food to the women's shelter," she said. "But, why do you want to hand out money to a bum? You know he's going to go buy booze with that, don't you?" Grace was emphatic.

Unbeknownst to Colleen, Grace spoke from first-hand experience, as she recalled in her mind the fading image of someone she knew long ago, whose desire for the bottle outweighed all other necessities and responsibilities.

Colleen was unfazed by Grace's grilling. "I just felt like I needed to," she replied. But she could tell that her go-to phrase wasn't going to settle the girl's heart.

"It's like this," Colleen said, without taking her eyes off the road. She paused for a moment, deciding to take a different tact with her explanation. "Do you know why I liked you before I even met you?" Grace didn't know what to make of the question, and she didn't answer. Colleen continued. "I love your name. I think you have one of the best names there is."

"My name?" Grace asked, confused. "What does that have to do with giving a homeless guy money?"

"Your name has meaning. Grace has lots of meanings, actually. But one of my favorites is kind of like a special favor, especially a favor that isn't deserved." She could tell Grace wasn't any closer to understanding her intentions. "Sometimes, people just need to be shown a little grace. That's all. The fact that I gave that man back there ten dollars might be more valuable to him than the money itself. Maybe he needed someone to show him some grace."

"I guess I get it," Grace said, as they pulled into the parking lot of the women's shelter. "But I still think it's a little weird."

"Well," Colleen began as she parked the car, "I've experienced so many undeserved favors in my life, it makes it easier for me to give a few back. I think one day, you'll understand better."

Chapter Twelve

PURPOSE

TUESDAY AFTERNOON SEEMED LIKE AN odd time to tell someone they no longer had a job, but that's when it happened to Melody. She knew business had been slow. Sales were down. One of the drug companies' products had been pulled from the market within the last month. But it still came as a surprise.

Ryvex Pharma was Melody's first job after college. She had worked there for six years, and it had been the perfect job for her. She worked in human resources for the medium-sized company in a six-story building in the downtown area of the nearest big city to Springville. Her apartment was perfectly situated halfway between work and her parent's house, a twenty-minute drive to both.

She had seen lots of employees come and go in six years' time, but she had lots of friends who had been with her there from the beginning. When it was time for budget cuts and to lay off salespeople, her department was affected.

She was sitting at her desk when her boss came by around 4:00 p.m. "Melody, can I see you in my office for a minute?" he asked. She had seen this kind of thing around her enough times to know what was coming, and her heart sank.

The layoff was effective right away, but the severance package was very generous. As Melody walked to her car, carrying a box full of desk knickknacks and framed pictures of her family, she thought about how quickly life can change. Seeing the nameplate that used to rest on her desk now riding in the front seat of her car was surreal.

As unexpected as it was, the shock of what happened wore off before she even got home. She was sad, but there weren't any tears. She felt confused, but not hopeless.

"What would Mama do?" Melody pondered aloud inside her apartment, while eating Rocky Road straight from the container. She hadn't yet called her mother. She needed time to process it for herself. *I know what Mama would do,* she thought.

Melody picked up her Bible.

And we know that all things work together for good to those who love God, to those who are the called according to His purpose.[5]

Interestingly to Melody, it wasn't the assurance that everything would work out okay that inspired her about the verse. It was the last word—*purpose.*

What is my purpose? Do I have one?

Melody had always taken pride in her ability to be content, quite unlike her mother. She had a consistent satisfaction with her life, whatever the situation. Maybe it was because she had grown up watching her mother's never-ending search for purpose and meaning. Melody believed she honored God simply by being content with herself and with her circumstances, trusting in His plan to guide her.

She never felt like she had to prove herself to anyone. She thought back to her high school days, back when it seemed most girls would have done anything to be popular and gain approval from their peers.

---

5 Romans 8:28

But she was so confident in who she was, and in Whose she was, Melody never struggled with feelings of inadequacy.

An ended career, however, seemed like a reason to take inventory of life. It was time to evaluate the choices she had made, and Melody wondered if her confidence and contentment had led her to a place of unrealized potential.

Six years of my life, just gone, she thought. *Did I play it too safe? What if I had tried harder to make myself less expendable? Should I have been fighting all this time to climb higher on the corporate ladder?*

The framed pictures that once sat atop her office desk were now spread out on the coffee table in the living room of her apartment. Melody lounged on the couch, having traded the ice cream for a cup of tea, and stared at the pictures of her family while a game of *This is Your Life* played in her mind.

Purpose. What is purpose?

It took a long time of listening, but finally, in the stillness of her apartment, Melody felt God speaking to her. She sat in the quiet, with her eyes clinched shut, feeling a familiar electricity on her skin, and she soaked up the thoughts that were suddenly present in her mind.

Her realization was that there are seasons in life, each with its own purpose. She felt at peace, knowing she had, in fact, followed His plan for her life up to this point. There was no reason to question the path she had chosen. It had been chosen for her, and she basked in the feeling of Divine absolution that cradled her.

Ever since she was very young, Melody had strived to live out Micah 6:8: "to do justly, to love mercy, and to walk humbly with your God." She had always felt like that was enough. And she was right. It was still enough. But she felt a new season was coming, one that would expand her application of those words. It was time to take the lessons she had learned from the past season and build on them.

The peace she felt stayed in her memory, even as the feeling faded away, and a longing to better understand her purpose replaced it. She wondered if there were new ways she could "do justly" and how God might want her to live out the concept of "loving mercy." *Is there a different way to walk humbly in my relationship with God?* she questioned.

Melody stayed still and quiet again for a long time, waiting to hear answers to her questions. But the answers didn't come, nor would they that evening, because sometimes God chooses to show an answer, rather than to simply give it.

Melody decided to call her mother. Colleen had instilled in her enough self-confidence to handle difficulties on her own, but she had also provided enough love and encouragement to make Melody crave her comfort when things were bad.

On the phone, Colleen was equal parts sympathetic and excited. She had a way of looking on the bright side of everything.

"I'm so sorry, baby girl," she said over and over as Melody relayed the story of getting the bad news. Even though Melody already knew it, she was comforted when her mother pointed out what a blessing the change might be.

"How nice that you can take a break from working! Just think of what all you can do!" Colleen said. "You'll be okay without a paycheck for a little while. And Daddy and I can help out some if you need."

Melody smiled. It was comforting to have people she could count on to help her, no matter what happened. Along with her parents, she knew she had a brother and sister-in-law she could lean on, too.

"Since you have free time now, maybe you can come help me and Grace sometime," Colleen told her. "I know she would like to meet you, and you know I'd love to spend more time with my only daughter! Don't worry, baby girl. God's got a purpose in all this."

Chapter Thirteen

DISPLACEMENT AND EMILY DICKINSON

GRACE WOULD NEVER HAVE ADMITTED that she was happy to visit Mr. Hartman's house again. There was just something about it—something about him—that she liked, although she couldn't describe why, even to herself.

As Colleen's SUV turned onto the gravel driveway, Grace surveyed the yard and the trees, the front porch, and the windows of the little house. She imagined, for a moment, Mr. Hartman's son as a little boy, looking out of those windows, waiting for his father to come home. She imagined him climbing the apple trees and jumping off the porch steps. She wondered if Mr. Hartman imagined those kinds of things, too.

Colleen was unaware that Grace had an announcement to make as soon as they stepped inside the house. She had forgotten about Grace's homework assignment, but Grace had not forgotten.

"Sequoyah created a writing system for the Cherokee language in 1821, which made it possible for the Cherokee people to send letters to one another and print newspapers in their own language." Grace's greeting to Mr. Hartman was a surprise to him, too. He wasn't thinking about the homework, either, but he was impressed.

"Well, now," he said. "Somebody's been doing some reading! Good for you!"

Grace smiled at the compliment, only briefly, still not willing to show too much emotion.

"I think you deserve a cookie," he said. "Go on in there in the kitchen and get some of those gingersnaps out of the jar." Something about the way she walked when she left the room to retrieve her reward made it obvious to Colleen that, while almost a woman, Grace was still much more of a little girl.

Colleen winked at Mr. Hartman. "I think she likes you."

"What's not to like?" he said, winking back.

"Mr. Hartman," Colleen said as Grace came back into the room with a handful of cookies, "I know you've always enjoyed a good book. I thought you might like for Grace to read to you today while I tidy up a bit in here. I've got a couple here you can choose from, or maybe you have one of your own you'd like for her to read."

"Let's try this one." Mr. Hartman pointed to a book of poetry with a crimson-colored cover. Colleen hadn't told Grace that one of Mr. Hartman's favorite activities during her regular visits was to listen to her read. His eyesight was failing, and having someone read to him brought him joy. Colleen had read him several chapters in the Bible, a couple of suspense novels, some educational non-fiction, and even a comic book or two. But poetry was his favorite.

Grace sat down on the sofa closest to Mr. Hartman's wheelchair. She finished chewing hurriedly, then opened the book to start reading. A stray crumb fell from her mouth, and she quickly brushed it off page one before she began.

Mr. Hartman closed his eyes and listened to a poem, then another, then another. On the fourth, he stopped her.

"You're a very good reader, Grace," he said sincerely. "But you've got to put more emotion into it. Poetry is supposed to make you feel something—good or bad, doesn't matter, as long as you feel *something*."

Grace looked at him with her mouth open. Her first instinct was to protest, to talk back, even to put the book down and refuse to read any more. She wasn't insulted, but she had been challenged to feel things she didn't want to feel and by this man she barely knew. Yet, as she had found the first time she met him, she couldn't dismiss him as she could most people. She cleared her throat and started reading, this time with feeling.

If I can stop one heart from breaking,

I shall not live in vain;

If I can ease one life the aching,

Or cool one pain,

Or help one fainting robin

Unto his nest again,

I shall not live in vain.

"Dickinson," Mr. Hartman announced, recognizing the author. "Fine words. Gives us all something to think about, doesn't it?" Grace only nodded in response. The words had moved her, too, but the emotional language that came from her lips had left her feeling naked.

"We all have a purpose," he said.

Somehow, the poem had struck a chord in Mr. Hartman's memory. He started talking about his time in the military. He talked about his late wife, Maryann—how they met at the diner in town when he was home on leave. He told her about Robert, Junior, whom they called Bobby. Grace learned that Bobby was a star baseball player in high school and that he loved cars.

Grace listened as Mr. Hartman talked for almost twenty minutes straight. She enjoyed his stories, and the joy on his face as he brought his family back to life with words made her feel peaceful. His entire demeanor was relaxed, and his eyes were bright. Talking about his family made him feel like they were still there with him. Having a new audience in Grace gave him the opportunity to talk about memories he carried in his heart, but never spoke aloud, since Colleen had already heard his stories and had known Maryann and Bobby when they were living. When he seemed finished saying all he needed to say, Grace waited a few seconds, then spoke up.

"Mr. Hartman?"

"What is it, child?"

"I read more about the Cherokee, besides just about Sequoyah."

"I'm glad of that. The more you learn, the better. What did you learn?"

"I read some really awful stuff." She paused, and he waited. "Why did we push them out like that?"

Mr. Hartman thought for a long while. "First off, we can't say *we* did any of that. You and I weren't there, and we didn't have anything to do with it. Feel sorrowful. Feel sympathy. Feel determined to never let injustice such as that happen again. But you should never, ever feel guilty for something you had no control over." The old man spoke with more conviction than Grace had ever heard in her fourteen years.

"But if you want to know why it happened," he continued, "it was selfishness." Mr. Hartman was still emphatic. "Just plain, old, ugly selfishness." The staccato of each adjective brought them to life. "People get themselves in a heap of trouble whenever they start thinking and feeling like their thoughts and feelings are more important than somebody else's, or worse yet, they just don't even think about other people at all."

Grace thought about Mr. Hartman's answer for a while, and he gave her some time to process it. She had spent a lot of time and energy dwelling on the injuries she had suffered in life, but she had given little thought to her own tendency toward selfishness.

Colleen came into the living room, carrying a tray of lemonades, and Grace was thankful for the interruption of her thoughts. They spent the rest of the time in friendly, casual, easy conversation. Colleen talked about the game show audition coming up and about how she had been preparing by reading *Trivial Pursuit* cards every night. She shared some of the fun facts she had learned.

"Did you know a twelve-sided, two-dimensional shape is called a dodecagon?" she asked. They didn't. "Well, do you know that bats are the only mammal that can fly?" Mr. Hartman knew that one, but it was new information to Grace.

They talked about the town Independence Day celebration coming up on Friday. Colleen suggested that she and Harvey could take Mr. Hartman to see the fireworks. For such a small town, Springville had the most impressive display in five surrounding counties.

"I appreciate it, Colleen, but I'll pass. I heard and saw my share of big booms overseas," Mr. Hartman said.

They sipped their glasses of lemonade, with the conversation eventually turning to the weather.

On the car ride back to the children's home, Colleen complimented Grace on her interaction with Mr. Hartman. "I think you were a big help today, Grace," she said.

"I didn't do anything. Just read some poems and let him talk for a while."

"Honey, you did more for him than you know."

Chapter Fourteen
BECKY

JULY HAD ALREADY SHAPED UP to be a busy month for Colleen. She had the town Independence Day celebration, Harvey's birthday, her work with Grace, and the game show audition coming up soon. It was getting difficult not to spring up like a jack-in-the-box every time she thought about the audition. Anticipation was her constant companion.

Sitting in the car just before the Ladies' Ministry League meeting, she looked at the calendar on her phone. She double-checked commitments for the next two months, thought about what else she could squeeze into her schedule, and consulted "the list." The list was a small notebook Colleen kept in her purse. She used it for keeping ideas of things she wanted or needed to do or just random things that popped into her brain. It was really a notebook of many things, but she called it her list; and she referred to it often for planning and remembering.

The list wouldn't have made much sense to anyone else that happened to read it. On one page was a grocery list; on another, the beginning of a poem Colleen was writing; on another, a favorite Bible verse; on another, a budget for the week; and, on another, some ideas for plans, like soap-making. The *future plans* page of her book also listed *salsa dancing; painting; girl trip to Biltmore; take Prairie to the zoo;* and *hike the Mountains-to-Sea Trail.* Colleen thought that after the game show was over, and her work with Grace was finished, she might tackle different stretches of the marked trails that stretched across the whole state. *I've still got plenty of spring in my step,* she thought. *Fall would be the perfect time.*

Colleen scanned the page again, then penciled in *zip-lining* at the bottom, so she wouldn't forget about it. Her heart raced with excitement, as she imagined zipping through the trees so high up from the ground.

It was time for the meeting to start, so she refreshed her mauve lipstick, checked for mascara smudges, and made her way to the fellowship hall, taking a moment to admire the row of bright pink azaleas in front of the building.

The ladies were abuzz about their booth at the Springville Freedom Celebration, discussing who had already baked their cakes and who was working which shift. As a group, they planned to bake twenty-five cakes to auction off, and the proceeds would go to the general fund of the Ladies' Ministry League. Colleen had made a Coconut Crème Cake and a Pineapple Upside Down Cake every year for more years than she could remember, and they always brought in the most money. Baking the Fourth of July cakes was on the top of her to-do list for the afternoon.

The Independence Day celebration was the highlight of the year for the town. Most people in Springville held patriotism as a virtue that never went out of style. Bigger than the Christmas parade by double, the annual Fourth of July parade would roll down Main Street mid-morning; then the feature event with vendors, games, music, and food would run from late afternoon to evening, culminating with the fireworks show just after dark. The obvious purpose of the event was to celebrate the birth of the nation; the secondary purpose was to encourage traffic to Springville's downtown area, which was quickly becoming a ghost town, just like the rest of Main Street, USA.

Colleen greeted several friends as she made her way across the fellowship hall.

"Hey, Peggy! How's your mama doing?"

"Helen, I want to hear about your trip to the Poconos later!"

"Mrs. Foster, it's so good to see you! I'm glad you're feeling better! We've sure been missing you."

When Colleen found an empty chair in the circle of friends, she was surprised to find Becky Johnson sitting in the chair beside hers. Becky had never been to one of their meetings before.

"Well, hey there!" Colleen greeted her.

Before Colleen had a chance to find out why Becky was there, Marsha called the meeting to order. Becky smiled at Colleen and shook her hand, while Marsha greeted everyone and called on one of the ladies to say the opening prayer.

As usual, the group discussed the efforts of the week, including an update from Colleen about the meal she and Grace had prepared for the women's shelter and the visit with Mr. Hartman. Everyone seemed pleased that the poor girl from the children's home was getting an opportunity to learn to work hard and help others, and they appreciated Colleen's time and effort.

Marsha spoke up. "I'm happy to have my cousin, Becky, here today from Oak Grove Children's Home. I'd like for her to tell us how she feels our ongoing community outreach effort is going."

Even though Colleen had chosen to work alone, the project was still an effort of the LML, so *our* was an appropriate pronoun. But it caught Colleen off-guard. She had taken ownership of the project. It was difficult to think about it belonging to anyone else, too, and she hoped her face didn't give her away.

"It's nice to be here. Thank you for having me," Becky began. "Based on what I've seen and heard from our resident, I agree with Colleen that this effort has been very successful so far. On behalf of Oak Grove, we appreciate your support, and we look forward to partnering with you on other projects in the future."

As it turned out, Becky didn't talk much about Grace specifically. She was there, primarily, to talk about other volunteer opportunities for the group and individuals. She also asked the ladies to bring their friends and families to the information booth at the Springville Freedom Celebration.

"Oak Grove Children's Home will have a booth at the event tomorrow, as well. We want to promote awareness about our facility and our mission, and we want to encourage people to donate, to volunteer, and to consider fostering or adopting." Unintentionally, Becky's face morphed from encouraging and smiling to somber as she reported on the statistics. "There are over ten thousand children in our state currently in foster care. And personally, if I can be direct, I think it should be a mission of the Church to reduce that number."

When the meeting adjourned, most of the ladies stayed to talk. Many approached Becky to learn more about volunteering. Her short speech had inspired them. When she was free, Becky went over to Colleen, who was waiting for her.

"Colleen, what you've done so far with Grace has been remarkable. After only two weeks, the houseparents are telling me they see an improvement in her attitude! And I've seen it myself. I'm not sure how you've done it!" Becky said.

Colleen felt herself blush, and she started to respond, but Becky wasn't finished. "I do have a concern, though, that I didn't express before. Do you have a few minutes to talk?"

It took Colleen aback, how quickly the look on Becky's face shifted from joy to worry. "Sure. What's on your mind?" Colleen said. "I think Grace is actually starting to enjoy the project. She hasn't opened up a lot, but I think she's really learning what it means to help others." Colleen was nervous about what Becky was going to say, and she rambled.

"Please don't get me wrong," Becky said. "I believe this is working out to be a really positive thing for Grace. Truly. I don't have any concerns about your time with her." She paused. "My concern is about what happens when the forty hours of service is over. I know Grace doesn't show it, but I think she is developing an attachment to you. I just worry about her getting hurt."

Colleen had to admit it to herself that she hadn't given the question any thought. So far, it had been only two weeks. Just four days. Ten hours. They had finished a quarter of their scheduled time together, and Grace wasn't on "the list" for future plans.

It wasn't that Colleen was looking forward to being finished with the project. It wasn't that she planned to *not* be involved with Grace when the project was over. She simply hadn't thought about it.

"When I had the idea of getting Grace involved with your church group," Becky continued, "I envisioned it as a more collaborative effort. I assumed she would have more interaction with different women. But since you've been so generous to volunteer your time toward *all* the service hours with Grace, we have to consider how she will feel when her *punishment* is over, and you two aren't spending time together anymore."

Colleen admired Becky. It was obvious that her role as director of the children's home was more than a job. She genuinely cared for the children. Colleen thought about the similarities between Becky's mission and her own, when she had so protectively cared for the residents of the nursing home.

Colleen didn't have a great answer for Becky, but she gave a truthful one.

"Like I said before, I just feel like I need to do this." Colleen sighed. "But I see where you're coming from. And I never want to cause that girl any harm."

"So, you'll get some of the other ladies to help? Maybe alternate weeks?"

"No!" she said, a little too quickly. "I mean . . . I really feel like I'm supposed to spend this time with Grace. And I really am grateful for the opportunity to help her complete her service hours."

Colleen searched for the words that would put Becky's mind at ease.

"If you're worried that she's getting too attached, I don't think that will cause a problem. When the project is over, I'm sure it won't be the last I see of her."

Becky could hear the sincerity in Colleen's voice, and she had no reason to doubt her. She simply had to trust that a greater plan was at work.

"Okay," she said. "Thanks for reassuring me. I just want to make sure we do what's best for Grace."

Chapter Fifteen

INDEPENDENCE DAY

ON FRIDAY MORNING, THE DAY of the Springville Freedom Celebration, Colleen's phone rang early, right as she sat up in bed and her bare feet touched the cool, wood floor. The ring had a different sound to it, a tone that said, *This is not good news.* It was a call that would change the weekly routine she had known for some time.

"Colleen, I'm sorry to call you so early," the voice on the other end of the line said. There was no need for the voice to identify himself. Colleen recognized her pastor, and experience told her right away what kind of call it was.

"I wanted to let you know that Robert Hartman passed away last night," the pastor said gently. "His nurse, Leigh, found him just now, peaceful in his bed."

Colleen immediately breathed a prayer for the young nurse as Preacher Whitefield continued speaking. She had no idea that finding Mr. Hartman was Leigh's first experience with death as part of her job or that her prayer for peace and comfort was needed so desperately.

As with Grace, Mr. Hartman's charm had drawn the nurse in. She had worked with him for six months, and during that time, they had grown close.

Leigh had started her shift earlier than normal that day, so she could leave early to get to the town celebration. She would be much too grieved, however, to attend the celebration at all.

Colleen thanked the pastor for calling as she sat back down on the edge of the bed. She held the phone in one hand and rested her head in the other. In all her years, she had received many calls like this from the pastor about church family who had gone on. This one was especially hard.

Even as the sadness gripped her heart, Colleen admired her pastor's eloquent speech. He had delivered this kind of news more times than he could count, and he had an inspired way with words in difficult situations.

Colleen was heartbroken, but the sad news also brought a sense of relief. It had been difficult to watch time and sickness drain away her long-time friend's strength and ability. It had pained her to see him live out his days in his house alone.

After she hung up the phone, she played out the most beautiful scene in her mind. She pictured Mr. Hartman, reunited with his wife and son, running into the open arms of Jesus. She shed a single tear, and she whispered thanks for the privilege of having Mr. Hartman as a friend.

Colleen's peace was suddenly shaken.

Oh, no! Grace! she thought. *I have to tell Grace. If I wait until I see her next week, she won't trust me at all. She needs to know sooner than later.*

Colleen had seen the light in Grace's eyes when she talked about Mr. Hartman, even though she had had only a couple visits with him. Colleen had known him for most of her life. Grace had known him for two weeks. Still, she feared that, to a fragile teenager like Grace, it would be a difficult loss to bear.

Having Grace visit with Mr. Hartman had never really been about helping him. It had been more about reaching Grace. Colleen knew that, to a young girl without a father, the old man's gentle spirit, wisdom, and caring nature would be endearing.

Colleen's brain scrambled to figure out what she should do. Michael would be at the door any minute with Prairie. They all planned to go to the celebration together later in the afternoon.

I need to call Becky, she thought. *She has to decide how to tell Grace.*

Colleen didn't know if Becky would be in the office on the holiday. If she did, she wouldn't be in for a couple more hours.

In the middle of her panic, Michael delivered a welcomed distraction to his mother in the form of a cuddly baby. With Prairie in the house, the stresses of the morning eased, and everything seemed brighter. Hearing her little voice say "Gammy" over and over was exactly what Colleen needed.

Near mid-morning, Colleen called Becky and let out a sigh of relief when she answered her office phone. At first, Becky wasn't sure how to handle the situation either.

"Oh, dear," Becky said after hearing the news. "I wonder how she'll take it."

"I guess there's no way to know until we tell her. But I wish I knew how to make it easy," Colleen said.

Becky agreed. "I don't know if it would be better coming from me or from you or from the counselor on staff here. It's so important to go about this the right way."

As they talked it over, Prairie played happily on a mat on the floor, oblivious to her grandmother's burdens.

Becky finally decided that she would be the one to tell Grace about Mr. Hartman's passing and that the service project would be put on hold for one week. The unforeseen circumstances made Becky second-guess the punishment.

"Maybe I should just cut her a break and call this off altogether," Becky said. "What she did wasn't even all that bad in the first place.

It was just that she had been in trouble so many, many times before."
Her voice had a tone of desperation. "We needed to find a way to get
her attention and try to teach her."

Becky had forgotten that Colleen didn't know why Grace was in
trouble to begin with, but she didn't elaborate.

Her voice was pained as she talked through options for her ward.
"I always want what's best for these kids," she said. "But the truth is,
sometimes I just don't know what that is."

Colleen wanted to reassure her, but she was careful to tread lightly.
It was ultimately Becky's choice to continue the arrangement or to
forget about it.

"Honey, listen. I'd still like to finish the remaining hours with
Grace," Colleen said. "Maybe she and I can start meeting just one day
a week, on Tuesdays, but for a longer period of time. Since she's still
on summer break, maybe it would work. We can devote all our efforts
to helping the women's shelter, just on Tuesdays."

Becky thanked Colleen for her devotion to the project.

"I think that will work," she said. "We'll at least keep trying."

Colleen hung up the phone and cradled Prairie in her arms. Despite
the sweet comfort of baby cuddles, worry still wracked her mind.
Maybe I should have gone over there to tell her myself, she thought. *I wish
I knew how she was going to take it.*

Around lunchtime at Oak Grove Children's Home, Becky called
Grace into her office. *What did I do this time?* Grace wondered.

Unlike her usual way, Becky got straight to the point. She handled the
situation like ripping off a Band-aid, but with as much sympathy and com-
passion as she could. When Grace heard the news, she looked for a moment
as if she had been punched in the gut. But the poker face quickly returned.

"That's too bad," she said. "He was a pretty neat old guy."

Unlike Grace, Colleen had the benefit of many distractions for the rest of the day. She went to the celebration as planned and even worked her scheduled shift at the LML booth. By the end of the auction, her cakes had again brought in the most money, and one even set a record at fifty-eight dollars.

Colleen and Harvey left before the fireworks, though, and she crashed into her recliner as soon as she got home. During the busy day, Colleen barely had time to grieve. Now, in the quiet, she could reflect and pay tribute to Mr. Hartman.

How fitting it was that he passed on Independence Day, she realized. Mr. Hartman had fought in Korea and in Vietnam. He had counted his freedom among the most precious gifts bestowed on him by the Creator. Now his body was free, released from the physical constraints it had known.

She thought about his love for books and the wisdom he had passed on to many. She thought about his stories of Maryann and Bobby. She thought about how much she would miss their visits. But mostly, she thought about how blessed she was to have known him.

While Colleen reflected on her friend's legacy, a young girl in a house just a few miles away sat by the window in the room she shared with three other girls. The other children had gone to the fireworks show, but Grace had stayed behind to grieve alone. The words of Emily Dickinson resonated in her mind.

I shall not live in vain.

The booming of colorful explosions nearby muffled the sounds of her heartache; and for the first time in a very long time, Grace let tears escape from her dark brown eyes.

Chapter Sixteen

A MEMORIAL AND A PARTY

MR. HARTMAN'S MEMORIAL WAS ON Monday. A gray sky matched the mood of the mourners as they bade farewell to the kind and gentle man.

Most of the attendees were members of the church, where Mr. Hartman had served the Lord and had grown in his faith. They gathered there to honor him and pay tribute to a life well-lived.

Colleen thought the Springville VFW post did a wonderful job carrying out traditional military honors. Per Mr. Hartman's wishes, the funeral was held in his own backyard, and his beloved mountains were in view behind the line of uniformed veterans during the twenty-one-gun salute. The goose-bump-covered arms of everyone there attested to the beauty of it.

The only awkward moment of the solemn day was right before the service began when someone from the funeral home asked the pastor to whom the burial flag should be presented. Mr. Hartman hadn't included that detail in his will, and there was no next-of-kin to receive the honor.

"I think you should have it," Pastor Whitefield suggested to Colleen. He knew the bond they had shared. She was probably the closest person to Mr. Hartman.

At first, she felt honored by the thought; but as much as Colleen loved him, it didn't feel right for her to claim it. It was too special, too significant. She didn't feel worthy.

"Pastor," she said, "why don't we keep it at the church, for everyone to remember him and be proud of his service? We can find a nice display box for it and put it somewhere it will be noticed."

The pastor agreed that it was a good idea, but Colleen was still the one to receive the flag during the service. When she took the cotton banner in her hands, she experienced one of the greatest feelings of pride she had ever known. It was an incredible honor to hold the physical representation of her friend's bravery and patriotism.

Someone missing from the gathering of mourners was Grace. Becky had offered to take her, but she had said "no thanks," as if turning down an invitation to dinner. Grace had invested too much time and energy building a façade of indifference, and she didn't want it torn down by being caught shedding tears for someone she barely knew.

The week was a whirlwind of emotion for Colleen. She continued to grieve, but it was also a time of celebration. Harvey's birthday was just two days after the memorial.

Birthdays were always a big deal in their home. It didn't matter how old the birthday person was, there would at least be a cake, candles, and the singing of the "Happy Birthday Song." More often than not, parties included balloons and noisemakers, too. The Hills enjoyed celebrating each year of life.

This year, Harvey's birthday party would include an extra treat.

"Mama, I'm looking forward to meeting your little friend," Melody told Colleen, who was busy mixing frosting with a hand mixer.

"I'm so glad she agreed to come! I was worried she wouldn't," Colleen said. She was shouting over the noise of the mixer more loudly than was necessary. "I think she will enjoy it. After the sadness of the week, I just thought it was a good idea."

Melody hovered nearby, waiting to lick the beaters as soon as her mother finished the frosting. That's what she did when she was in Mama's kitchen.

Melody and Colleen scuttled around like mice, putting the finishing touches on the party. "Oh, I want this to be nice!" Colleen said. Kimberly, Michael, Prairie, and Grace would be there at 7:00 p.m. Sherrill had planned to come, too, but she threw out her back picking cucumbers and had to cancel.

By 6:45 p.m., they had inflated all the balloons and hung all the streamers. Harvey's favorite meal of meatloaf, coleslaw, and mashed potatoes was on the table, and a three-layer carrot cake waited on the kitchen counter. Colleen and Melody made a great fanfare, announcing to the guest of honor that he was finally allowed to come out of the garage.

Harvey entered the dining room and said the same thing he always said, every single year. "Wow! Look at all this! Is it somebody's birthday?"

Melody hugged her Daddy and laughed. His lame jokes never got old.

"Daddy, it's hard to believe you're sixty-four," said Melody. "You don't look a day over sixty-five." She had a touch of her father's sense of humor and his mischief, too.

Harvey was appreciative of his wife and daughter's hard work, and he was excited to see the rest of his family. He also looked forward to meeting Grace. On the Tuesdays Grace had been there, he happened to not be home, but Colleen had told him so much about her, he felt like he knew the girl well.

Grace arrived right on time, and she was surprised that it was Harvey who greeted her at the door. She was even more surprised when he grabbed her at once in a big bear hug.

"Hello! Thank you so much for coming to my party!" He released the girl. "I'm so glad to meet you. I'm Colleen's husband, Harvey."

Always short on words and big on affection, Harvey hadn't given a second thought to greeting the girl in such a way. The hug had the effect of making Grace feel warm and welcomed and making her want to run away at the same time.

She smiled at the tall, broad-shouldered man. It was a genuine smile, but the only thing she could manage to utter was a weak, little, "Hi."

Colleen entered the room, still wearing her apron, smeared with frosting. She was surprised to see that Grace had dressed up for the occasion. "Well, don't you look pretty, honey!" Colleen said. "My, my, my! Come on in, and make yourself at home."

The girl, who wore a navy, knee-length party dress with matching lace overlay, made her way to the sofa and sat down in a noticeably more ladylike manner than she had the first time she visited. One of her roommates had French-braided her hair, a flattering look on the young girl.

Grace was nervous being around new people, but she hid it well. When a young woman with a peachy complexion and straight, dark-blonde hair came in, she recognized her at once from the pictures on the mantel.

Colleen introduced Grace to Melody, and they shook hands. "Glad you could make it, Grace," Melody said. "I love your dress!"

Grace beamed. She was glad she had decided to wear it, and she was glad her hosts didn't know it was the only one she owned.

Michael and his family arrived soon after, and Grace watched from the sofa as everyone exchanged hugs. She studied, noticing that three newcomers and three original party-goers totaled nine new hugs in a matter of a couple minutes. She didn't mind the emotional scene, but she did find it strange.

The smell of Colleen's cooking coming from the dining room was wonderful, and it was making her hungry. She didn't have to wait much longer, though. Colleen herded everyone to the table, so the party could officially begin, introducing Grace to the rest of the family as they took their seats—Harvey and Colleen at each end; Michael, Kimberly, and Prairie on one side; and Grace and Melody on the other.

Normally, Harvey said the blessing, but because it was his birthday, Michael volunteered. It was tradition to offer a special blessing for the guest of honor, and Michael relished the opportunity.

He was an articulate orator, and his voice carried a silky southern tone that charmed people anew with each lilt and inflection. As she listened to Michael's words with her head bowed in respect, Grace realized she had never heard praying like this before.

At the children's home, they recited "God is Great" before every meal. It was quick. It was habit. It was the only prayer she'd ever really heard, except for some she'd caught in sappy movies.

She thought about some of her friends from the home who went to church. It was their choice. Grace never went. *I wonder if they hear prayers like this there,* she thought.

One reason the style of Michael's prayer was foreign to Grace was that it contained so much emotion. Strong emotion had been her nemesis for a long time.

Michael prayed as if every word carried power and as if God were sitting right in the middle of the dining room table. It made Grace squirm in her seat.

She had already lowered her guard just by being there. Even from the beginning of the project, she had worked hard to squelch the bad attitude, to make things go smoothly. The party was an even bigger step. It was her attempt to be friendly, an attribute she normally held onto like a rare coin. But during the prayer, she started to wonder if this unusual party, with bear hugs from strangers and conversations with the invisible Almighty, was more than she could handle. Grace felt like they were asking her to write checks her bank of emotions couldn't cash.

The prayer didn't last forever, though, and the meal and, especially, the cake, turned out to be worth the strain on her emotional resources. Just like she had never heard prayers like Michael's, she had also never tasted food like Colleen's. It wasn't just delicious; it was strangely comforting, like hugging a teddy bear or talking with a friend. She didn't understand how a meal could make a person feel that way.

The dinner conversation was less demanding than Grace had anticipated. She relaxed and even laughed a little, especially when Prairie spit mashed potatoes all over her mother's blouse.

Melody kept Grace engaged in conversation more than anyone else. She tried to think of questions that weren't too intrusive but also wouldn't sound dumb to a fourteen-year-old.

"Grace, my mom says you are a natural cook. Do you have any other hobbies?"

The compliment about her cooking skills was a surprise, and it meant more to Grace than Melody or Colleen could have realized.

"Um, well, I draw sometimes," Grace answered. "I'm not great at it, but it's fun, I guess." She thought for a moment. "And I like helping out with the younger kids at Oak Grove sometimes. They're sweet." Grace could hardly believe she had admitted to enjoying anything to someone. Her modus operandi of indifference was destroyed, and she recognized it. There was no going back.

Everyone was looking at her, smiling with approval and interest. She tried to smile back, but she sank down in her chair instead.

A houseparent from the children's home came to pick up Grace soon after Harvey had opened his presents. He had received a new outdoor thermometer from Melody, two pairs of slacks for church from Colleen, and a goody basket of his favorite snack foods from Michael and Kimberly. Grace was embarrassed that she hadn't brought a gift, but Harvey had assured her that her being there was gift enough.

After Grace left, the family sat around talking and laughing until much too late. Prairie was sound asleep, so Michael and Kimberly took advantage of the chance to visit with his parents and sister.

"I think Grace had a good time," said Kimberly. "She may have been a little nervous at first, but she loosened up. I sympathized! I remember what it was like when Michael brought me over to meet y'all for the first time!" Everyone had a good laugh remembering their first meeting. Kimberly and Michael were so young back then, but Harvey and Colleen had known they would wind up getting married. It was parents' intuition.

Colleen leaned against the back of the sofa and threw her arm around her husband. She wondered if *intuition* was the right word for how sure she had been about volunteering with Grace. *No, that's not what it is,* she thought. Colleen knew it was much bigger than an intuitive feeling.

After Michael, Kimberly, and Prairie left the party, Harvey kissed his wife and daughter goodnight. "Us old people have to get our sleep, you know," he joked.

Melody didn't have the burden of getting up early to go to work, so she stayed a while longer. Mother and daughter enjoyed the quiet time together. They split one more piece of cake and sipped decaf, and they shared ideas about what Melody could do with her free time until she found another job.

"I can teach you how to knit," Colleen offered. "Or, what about taking a real estate class?"

"Maybe. I'll think about it."

As she gathered her things, preparing to leave, Melody had a new idea. It was something she had never considered before. It just occurred to her out of the blue.

"Mama, have you ever thought about making soap?"

Chapter Seventeen

THE SWEET SMELL
OF SUCCESS

ALONG WITH READING BOX AFTER box of trivia cards, Colleen spent the next few days researching different methods of making lavender soap. She found the internet, specifically YouTube, to be of significant help.

Thank you, Lord, for allowing us to have access to all this information, she prayed as she researched. *It never ceases to amaze me!*

She shared all her newfound knowledge with Melody, who was even deeper into the research and preparation than she was. The more Melody learned, the more interested she became. She saw that soap-making wasn't just a hobby; it was an art.

By Tuesday, Colleen had outfitted the kitchen to serve dual purposes—food preparation and soap-making. They were serious about the new venture.

When Harvey came into the kitchen and saw all the ingredients and accoutrements covering the table and every countertop, he didn't even ask questions. He just shrugged, winked at Colleen, and walked back into the living room to enjoy his coffee there instead.

Melody got there right after lunch, excited to be part of her mother's work with Grace. In preparation, she had purchased supplies she found over the weekend and delivered them to Colleen.

"Making soap to donate to the shelter was the perfect idea, Melody!" Colleen said, as she greeted her daughter with a firm side hug. Melody followed her into the kitchen.

"With sweet Mr. Hartman gone, I didn't know how Grace and I would fill her service hours." Colleen emptied the dishwasher while she talked. "And I think this will be a good distraction for her, too." She put some plates in the cabinet. "I don't know for sure, but I think his death really affected her. Maybe this will help lift both our spirits."

"Well, I'm ready for a distraction, too," Melody said. "I am so happy to be out of that apartment! I'm not used to spending so much time there by myself."

When Grace arrived, they explained the new venture to her. She seemed pleasantly surprised and genuinely excited about it, and she also seemed very pleased that Melody was joining them for the afternoon.

"Oh, these are pretty," Grace said. She picked up a bundle of dried lavender stems from the counter and put them to her nose, breathing their scent with a full, deep breath. "And they smell awesome!"

"Natural perfume!" Colleen chimed.

"And the soap we make with them is going to smell awesome, too!" Melody said. "But lavender doesn't just smell good. It also has healing properties. It can help calm you down when you're feeling anxious, and it can help you sleep. It even helps heal wounds."

"Just another wonder of creation!" Colleen exclaimed.

Grace ran her fingers over the tiny purple buds, sharing in Colleen and Melody's appreciation for the flower.

"Hey, do you think we can put some of the soaps we make into a little package, like a welcome gift?" she asked. "That might be nice for the women when they first get to the shelter."

Colleen and Melody stood looking at one another. It was a remarkable idea, and they were both impressed that Grace had offered it. It was hard to believe this was the same girl that had barely spoken to Colleen on her first visit.

"I think you might be on to something!" Colleen said. "What a thoughtful idea!"

It was a happy scene, the three of them standing in the middle of the quaint kitchen. The aroma of lavender overwhelmed them, and they shared a mutual, unspoken excitement about new possibilities.

At first, five hours in one day had sounded like a lot of time to fill. But, between the cooking *and* the soap-making *and* the delivery, it looked as if they would have no problem making effective use of the time.

Grace would work with Colleen one day a week now for the next six weeks, completing her service time right before a brand-new adventure began—high school.

Melody walked Grace through the plan for the day. "Today, we're keeping it pretty simple. We'll use this pre-made soap base that I got from the craft store. We just have to melt it, then mix in the flowers and the lavender oil and pour it into the molds to set! Easy peasy!"

Melody's excitement amused Grace.

"I have plans for *real* soap-making next week. Do you want to learn how to do it?"

Grace nodded in agreement, and Melody noticed that her pretty, brown eyes practically sparkled.

"We'll use olive oil, coconut oil, distilled water, and lavender. And the most important ingredient is lye. You can't make soap without lye! It will be great, but it does take more time."

Grace studied the soap base and the lavender. She looked around at bowls, spoons, pots, and molds spread around the kitchen. There were brown paper and twine for wrapping the bars of soap they would make. *This might be kinda fun,* she thought.

The only difficult part in procuring ingredients for the soap had been figuring out how much lavender they needed to buy. Since it was for a good cause and because they were friends of family, Sherrill's niece had given them a considerable discount on the flowers. Melody and Colleen bought more dried bunches than they could probably use in a lifetime of soap-making. They bought several fresh bunches to enjoy, too, and they spread them all over the house in mason jar vases.

They got to work and proved to be very industrious in the kitchen. After a couple of hours, they had produced even more bars than they had planned. It had set quickly, and there was still time left to work on Grace's idea to package the soap as welcome gifts.

Melody ran out to the nearest discount store to pick up the extra special supplies, while Grace and Colleen started cooking the baked spaghetti and preparing a salad.

Colleen held the strainer over the kitchen sink as Grace carefully poured the spaghetti noodles in it to drain. Colleen looked up; and through the steam that rose between them, she noticed a new and surprising expression on Grace's face. It was a genuine smile and a look of gratitude.

"It's been really fun today so far," Grace said.

"It has, hasn't it?" Colleen replied.

As soon as the glass dishes full of cheese-covered spaghetti were placed in the oven, Melody came bouncing back into the kitchen. She had thirty soft, white washcloths and a roll of silky, lavender-colored ribbon.

Melody and Grace sat at the table working on care packages while Colleen finished cooking. They each took a washcloth, wrapped three bars of the good-smelling soap inside, and tied the bundle. They first tied it securely with a piece of the strong twine, then tied it again with a piece of ribbon to add a touch of color to the gift.

Grace was proud of the result, but something seemed to be missing. "It needs a card!" she said. "We need some kind of card to explain what it's for or who it's from."

"Hmmm . . . " said Melody. "You are just full of good ideas today! Let me see what I can do."

Melody left the kitchen and came back soon with a stack of white cardstock paper, a hole punch, and a calligraphy pen she had gathered from her mother's office. Scissors were already on the table, so they had everything they needed.

"Maybe for next week, I can come up with a design on the computer and print out some cards. But I think handwriting them will work for now," Melody said.

First, they folded the paper to make guidelines for cutting, then they carefully cut little rectangles of the cardstock and folded them. Grace used the hole punch to make a hole for the ribbon to go through, in order to secure the cards to the packages.

Colleen came over to inspect the work and offer praise. "This is turning out even better than I thought it would! Grace, I'm proud of how hard you've worked today."

Grace looked up at Colleen and grinned to say *thank you,* then she glanced at Melody. For the first time, she noticed a resemblance in mother and daughter. They shared the same thin bridge of the nose and blue, almond-shaped eyes. The subject of genetics fascinated her, but Grace noticed much more than physical similarities. She had been watching them in the kitchen—how they spoke, how they moved. It was interesting how alike they were in mannerisms. She was suddenly embarrassed, realizing that watching family members interact made her feel like a scientist studying another species.

"What do you think we should write on our cards, Grace?" Melody asked.

"I don't know. Something nice. Something happy."

"I have an idea," said Melody. She pulled her phone out of her pocket to look up a verse of Scripture. "This makes me happy," she said. She read aloud from the first book by the apostle Peter. "Casting all your care upon Him; for He careth for you."[6]

Grace pondered the words. It sounded nice to her, but she didn't fully understand it. "Is the *Him* God?" she asked innocently. Colleen started to interject, but she stood back and let Melody handle the question.

"Yes!" said Melody, keeping the answer simple. "And you know what? I've thought about this verse a lot lately. It has been a tremendous help to me, so I think it might help those ladies at the shelter, too."

Grace reflected on the idea of something from the Bible being a *help*. She had always assumed it was just full of rules and stories of people that lived a long time ago.

"Why don't I write the verse on the inside of the cards, and you can put something on the front," Melody said. "How should we tell them who the gift is from?"

Grace smirked. She had already been thinking about it. "If we use all our initials for the name of the soap, it sounds like a car company!"

It took them a second to get the joke, then they all shared a giggle at the thought of soaps made by *GMC*.

"See? Names are important!" Colleen laughed. "Maybe we can use your name, Grace, in the name for our little venture. Do you remember how we talked about what your name means? We could write something like 'A Touch of Grace' or 'A Gift of Grace.'"

Grace was pleased by the thought. "It's pretty cheesy, but I like it! It needs something that describes the soap, too, though."

She put her elbow on the table and leaned her head against her fist while she thought. The room was quiet while they all brainstormed.

Grace took one of the cards and began to write on the front in her neatest, swirliest handwriting. When she finished, she tied the card on the package. The card read simply, "Grace & Lavender."

"Perfect!" Melody and Colleen said at the same time.

Grace and Melody finished enough packages to give to all twelve current residents of the shelter and the two staff members. Colleen had already loaded the food in the car, so Grace carried the basket full of soaps; and after saying goodbye to Melody, they headed for the shelter.

The feeling Grace had handing out a gift she had helped make with her own hands was remarkable. The smiles from the women and children warmed her heart in a way she had never known. *It's just soap*, she thought. *But it means more than that to them right now.*

After Colleen delivered Grace back to Oak Grove, she spent the short drive home thinking back on the successful afternoon. She hummed a happy tune while she reflected. *I so enjoyed watching Melody and Grace working together. Almost like sisters*, she thought. Then a new idea popped into Colleen's brain. She remembered Grace's question about the Bible verse and the look on her face when she heard Melody's answer. Colleen decided it was time to invite Grace to join them on Sunday morning at SCCC.

Chapter Eighteen
SUNDAY

ALL THE CHILDREN AT OAK Grove were allowed and encouraged to attend church if they chose to, but it wasn't required. On more than one occasion, Becky had gently asked Grace if she wanted to go. The answer was always no.

Several volunteers took children to church on the weekend, and Becky thought it was a wonderful thing. But she knew how fragile Grace really was. When Colleen asked to take Grace to church, it was hard for Becky to let go of the worry. She worried that Grace was becoming more and more attached to Colleen and that it would end up causing her heartache. As with most things, she had to weigh it out, and she eventually decided that the potential reward was greater than the risk.

"If she really wants to go with you, I can't possibly say no to that," Becky conceded.

Over the telephone, Colleen asked Grace about going to church, and not being able to see her face made it hard to read her. But since Grace said yes, Colleen had to trust that she genuinely wanted to go with her.

On Sunday morning, Colleen was more excited than a kid in a candy store. She was also a bit nervous. She wanted so badly for Grace's first church experience to be a positive one.

Colleen stood in front of the bathroom mirror, putting the finishing touches on her hair and makeup. *I'm being so silly,* she thought. *There's no reason in the world that it won't go well. Where in the world is my faith?*

Colleen turned down the collar on her silky, cream-colored blouse and straightened her pearls.

She thought back over the last few weeks. She realized that her time with Grace was becoming less and less about a community service project. She enjoyed being with her. It was no longer *just* about helping the poor orphan girl or *just* about doing her Christian duty.

At 10:30 a.m., Harvey and Colleen arrived to pick Grace up. She was ready and waiting out front with one of the houseparents, wearing the same navy dress she had worn to Harvey's birthday party. Her long hair was pulled neatly into a high pony tail.

As Grace slid into the backseat, Colleen noticed in the rearview mirror that she wore tinted lip gloss, and her cheeks were a light rosy shade.

"Good morning, sunshine!" Colleen greeted.

"Good morning."

Colleen read nervousness on the teenager's face. She tried to think of something to say that might put her at ease, but she found herself at a loss for words—such a rare occurrence that it surprised Colleen herself.

They quietly enjoyed the scenery as they rode. It was a beautiful summer morning, and Grace passed the twenty-minute ride silently naming the sights through neighborhoods, into the country, then in town. *Jogger, trees, historical marker, shaggy dog, trees, cows, church, silo, church, trees, goats, church, school, bank.* When they arrived at SCCC, Grace stepped out of the car and was immediately enveloped in clear, "Carolina blue" sky.

Harvey, Colleen, and Grace entered the sanctuary. Within those four walls, many lives had started anew. With a tall ceiling, stained glass windows that were high up from the floor, and an elevated platform across the front, the whole room had a lofty feel.

Harvey and Colleen made their way to their regular pew, in the middle of the right side of the church, with Grace following behind closely. She scooted into the pew close to Colleen; then realizing there was plenty of room, she slid away a little.

Grace noticed Colleen and Harvey smiling and throwing up their hands in greeting at other parishioners. She observed people who looked happy to be there, like they weren't pretending, and she thought it just might not be so bad.

It turned out Grace did enjoy the choir music. It was mostly bouncy and lively. The piano player put her whole body—not just her fingers and feet—into playing the instrument. Some people clapped their hands, and others tapped their choir books to the rhythm.

She also enjoyed hearing the children who came up front to recite their memory verses after the choir was finished. She especially liked the little boy who, determined to get his verse just right, repeated it from the beginning three times, until he pronounced the last word correctly.

The first part of the service was enjoyable, but the pastor's sermon left her feeling perplexed.

Pastor Whitefield preached from Psalm 68, verses three through six:

> But let the righteous be glad; Let them rejoice before God;
> Yes, let them rejoice exceedingly. Sing to God, sing praises to
> His name; Extol Him who rides on the clouds, By His name
> YAH, And rejoice before Him. A father of the fatherless, a

defender of widows, *Is* God in His holy habitation. God sets
the solitary in families; He brings out those who are bound
into prosperity; But the rebellious dwell in a dry *land.*

Grace didn't hear much of what the pastor said after the
Scripture reading. She just kept trying to process some of the words
and phrases he had read: *happy, joyful, father to the fatherless, sets the
lonely in families, rebellious.*

Am I rebellious? Am I lonely?

She couldn't answer her own questions, and Grace assumed that if
she couldn't answer them, then probably no one could. It made her feel
strangely non-existent. They were big thoughts for a fourteen-year-old,
but they hadn't been totally of her own consciousness.

Grace didn't show her confusion or give any hints about her intro-
spection. She sat quietly, looking at the pastor as he spoke, so Colleen
thought she was taking it all in and being very respectful. The irony
of the pastor's chosen passage, however, was not lost to Colleen, and
she wondered what effect it might have on the girl.

When the service was over, and Colleen and Harvey had introduced Grace to many more people than she felt comfortable knowing
in one day, Colleen motioned for her to follow. "I want to show you
something, honey."

Colleen took Grace back to the lobby through which they had
entered and to a far corner where a special shadow box and plaque
hung on the wall. "I thought you might want to see this. I helped to
get it hung up there this week. I didn't want to wait too long."

Grace read the plaque honoring Mr. Hartman's life and military career, and she saw the flag folded into a triangle, preserved behind glass
and displayed in his honor. She stared for a while, studying everything

about the memorial down to the weave of the flag, as if the tribute held something tangible of the man who had become her friend so quickly.

Colleen and Grace had managed to avoid the subject of Mr. Hartman's passing up until now, almost as if Grace had never met him. But Colleen felt she had to broach the subject somehow, to bring some closure to that facet of her relationship with Grace. She had no way of knowing how the girl would react.

Grace put one hand against the wall, as if it were holding her up. She closed her eyes tight, trying to shut out the world and the emotion which had overtaken her and wrapped her like a shroud.

Colleen instinctively reached to touch the girl's arm to comfort her, and Grace instinctively jerked her arm away as if the touch were poison. The entire exchange was a reminder to Colleen that Grace was, in fact, a very fragile child and that her reactions were unpredictable.

Grace turned and headed out the door and toward the car. Colleen didn't have to chase her, but she walked briskly to keep up. Harvey noticed the abrupt exit from a distance and soon caught up with them, not asking any questions.

They had already planned to take Grace back to the children's home right after church. That was the arrangement to which Becky had agreed, and Colleen was glad. She didn't know any way to help the girl, except by doing what she did best. Unlike the ride to church, Colleen found words to fill the silence on the way back.

"Grace," she started gently, "I can't wait to tell you on Tuesday about how my audition goes tomorrow. I'm so excited, I bet I won't even sleep tonight." Grace stared up at the roof of the car, not looking at anything. "Melody's going with me. She's going to drive." Colleen's tone was subdued as she studied Grace's face in the rearview mirror and tried to keep talking. "I wish I was meeting Rodney Vaughn. But, of course, that won't happen unless I get on the show."

Harvey could feel the tension in the car, but since Colleen wasn't talking about what was wrong, he figured he shouldn't either. He wanted to help lighten the mood, too.

"You just better not forget your dear, old husband if you meet Mr. Vaughn," he said. "Remember who's been putting up with you all these years. I know you think he's better looking than me."

"Better looking?" Colleen said, feigning disbelief. "No way!"

The couple smiled, but Grace didn't show any change in her demeanor.

Soon, they arrived at their destination, and Colleen escorted Grace toward the main entrance of the building. Heartbroken by the girl's silence and cold expression, Colleen needed to speak. "I'm sorry I upset you today," she said.

"You didn't," Grace said, and she picked up her pace to walk through the doors alone.

Chapter Nineteen

RISK AND REWARD

"I'M TELLING YOU, DAD, YOU should have seen her!" Melody exclaimed. "She was on fire!'

After the long drive home from Raleigh, Colleen and Melody sat in the living room, telling Harvey all about the day's events.

"I actually felt kinda bad for the other people auditioning. Mama was that good," Melody gushed.

"Oh, I wasn't that good," Colleen said sheepishly.

"Now, Collie, don't be so modest. Our girl is proud of you!" Harvey encouraged.

"Well, I do think I did pretty well. And it was so much fun! I haven't had that much fun in . . . I don't know when!" said Colleen. "They had it set up just like the real game, just the way it is on TV. Everything except Rodney Vaughn. But the little guy they had fill in for him did look a whole lot like him! And I did get lots of questions right."

"Tell him the best part of the story, Mama. Tell him!" Melody urged. She was practically bouncing up and down in the armchair.

"Oh, yeah! Can you believe there was actually a category called *Southern Cooking*? And another one was *Bible Literacy*!" Colleen slapped Harvey on the leg, harder than she meant to, in excitement. "It was like they wanted me to do well! I cleaned up on the cooking one, and I got four out of the six Bible questions!"

"It was so exciting to watch, Daddy," Melody added. "I wish you could have been there."

"Sounds incredible! So, you think you've definitely got a spot on the show?" Harvey asked with anticipation. Melody's excitement was infectious.

"Well, now, like I said, I have to meet with the producers for a one-on-one."

"But you know that's just a formality, Mama," Melody interjected. "They as much said so. I heard them."

"I know. I think it's just an extra step to make sure they aren't letting any nut jobs on television," Colleen chuckled.

"Oh, well," Harvey said with a smile, "it was a fun idea. Better luck next time."

Colleen ignored the joke. Melody snickered.

"It does seem fairly certain," Colleen admitted. "But I'm not counting my chickens until they hatch. Speaking of chickens, the agricultural fair is coming up, and I'm thinking about entering some preserves for the first time. What kind do you think I should try?"

"Mama, why are you changing the subject? This is something you have been off-the-charts excited about; and when it happens, you act like it's no big deal. You can't even enjoy this moment without chomping at the bit to start the next project on your list."

Harvey gave Colleen a raised-eyebrow look that said, *You know she's right.*

"Well, I don't know what you mean, baby. I am enjoying the moment. I enjoy every moment! I mean, why stop and smell the roses when you can sniff the whole garden, huh?"

Melody knew there was no arguing with her. Her logic was admirable in some ways, but Melody felt that her mother's approach to living wasn't as fulfilling as she tried to make herself believe. And Melody was quite certain it wouldn't be changing any time soon.

Getting back to the game show, Melody said, "Well, I enjoyed getting to play the part of the studio audience. I just tried not to cheer *too* much, so they wouldn't kick me out."

"Well, if I believed in good luck charms, I would say you are definitely mine! You were a great cheerleader, and I know it helped me."

"You would have done that well without me, but I was happy to be there. I hope I can go with you when you tape the show. And, Daddy, guess what? They said the shows that they are auditioning for now will be taped in late November and will air before Christmas. We could be spending Thanksgiving in L.A.!"

Colleen threw back her head and let out a big *Ha*, allowing herself to enjoy the thrilling thought.

"I'm surprised things move so quickly," Harvey said.

"They're moving right on time!" Colleen said matter-of-factly. "Everything in life does." She smiled at her husband, who understood and agreed with her faith in God's timing.

"Oh, and Mama . . . " Melody said. She paused dramatically, clasped her hands together, and looked at her mother with seriousness, exaggerating the importance of what she was about to say. "I think fig preserves would be best. They're the most . . . *interesting.*"

Chapter Twenty

ENLIGHTENMENT

COLLEEN SAT AT THE KITCHEN table, studying the container of lye and re-reading all the warnings on the label. In its original state, sodium hydroxide could be very harmful, but they were taking all the necessary precautions for using it. The risks were low when handled correctly, and the reward would be a batch of pure, cleansing soap.

The instructions clearly spelled out how to handle the substance safely without getting burned. *Wouldn't it be nice if people had similar labels?* Colleen thought. Her heavy sigh seemed to come all the way from her toes.

After the episode with Grace on Sunday, she didn't know what to expect the next time she saw her. She didn't know if she would still be upset or if she would even come at all. And she wondered if Becky had known that anything was wrong.

Colleen didn't want Becky to have any more reasons to worry about her project with Grace. As more time passed, Colleen became even more confident that, somehow, the Maker of all things had set this plan into motion and wanted her to carry it out.

She was glad when Grace showed up right after Melody arrived. The teenager was a bit more withdrawn than the week before, but, otherwise, there was no indication that anything had happened between them. Still, Colleen and Melody used kid gloves.

"Honey, we're making chicken pies today. What do you think about that?" Colleen asked.

"Sounds good."

"And I really need your help with this big batch of soap we're starting. I've never done it before, and I'm a little nervous," Melody said.

"All right."

"Before we get started, how about a snack?" Colleen offered.

"I just ate lunch."

It seemed to Colleen that today was going to be all business, much like the first time they had worked together over a month prior. It wasn't quite as bad as one step forward and two steps back, but any back-tracking was a disappointment to Colleen. She thought maybe she should have pushed Grace to talk about her feelings on Sunday, to get them out. In her imagination, Colleen could see the door behind which Grace kept all her hurt locked, but she just didn't know where to find the key.

Melody had assembled all the ingredients to tackle making soap from scratch. For now, they would cook lye, oils, and water in a crock-pot, on the other side of the room from where the food was cooking. There wouldn't be much more to do that day, other than to pour the soap into molds to set once it was finished cooking. Melody wanted to let it cure for a couple weeks before unmolding it.

It wasn't the same instant gratification as the melt-and-pour process, but Melody had the idea that committing to a longer process would, perhaps, represent to Grace that they wanted her to stick around. She didn't know if Grace would connect the dots in that way, but she hoped so.

They worked together to carefully measure and mix and stir soap ingredients while the chicken was on to boil. The smell in the kitchen was a strange mixture of boiled poultry and lavender.

Colleen and Melody kept trying to make conversation. They gave Grace the same run-down about the game show audition as they had given Harvey—about how well Colleen had done and the likelihood of her making it on television. Grace contributed a "that's great" and "pretty neat" here and there, but she was mostly quiet. When it was time to just let the soap cook, Melody had something to show Grace.

"I designed these and printed them out. What do you think?"

The new cards, on linen-colored paper, looked like packaging for soap sold in a real boutique. Melody had designed a beautiful logo for the front of the card. It had *Grace* arched across the top, a transparent ampersand on top of a picture of stems of lavender in the middle, and the word *lavender* straight across below that. On the inside was the same verse of Scripture they had handwritten the week before.

Grace was very impressed, and it made her feel important to see the name she had come up with printed so nicely on the front of the pretty card. "I really like it," she said genuinely, offering a hint of a smile. Melody and Colleen were both relieved to see it. Grace had a beautiful smile, and they didn't get to see it as often as either of them would have liked.

Grace's smile made another vision appear in Colleen's imagination. She saw Grace's heart and the door to it—not with one lock, but with many. She realized there wouldn't be just one key to unlocking Grace's heart to allow good things to enter. One of the keys was patience. Another key was definitely love, but she wondered if she could find the rest. And if she couldn't, who could?

It was time to work on the meal, and Colleen was excited for Grace to help her assemble the chicken pies. "This is one of my favorite recipes," she said. "I've made it for years and years."

"And it's one of my favorite things to eat!" Melody chimed. "It doesn't get much better than Mama's chicken pie, let me tell you!"

When Grace asked Colleen if the recipe was in her cookbook, it seemed that her mood had shifted, and they could relax.

"Yes, of course!" said Colleen. "See, it's right here." She turned to the page in her cookbook, and Grace started reading the list of ingredients aloud. She stopped mid-list and chuckled in a way they hadn't heard before.

"Boy, that's ironic," she said, the few words punctuated with sarcasm.

Her sudden change in tone surprised them, and Melody and Colleen looked at Grace, confused, wondering what would come next. She didn't elaborate.

"What's ironic, honey?" Colleen finally asked.

"That one of these ingredients is the reason I'm here."

She stood leaned up against the kitchen counter, staring at them, with arms folded, and Melody sensed an unspoken *duh* behind Grace's statement. All they could do was stare back.

"You know . . . 'cause of what happened at the grocery store," Grace prompted.

Colleen took a deep breath, then felt emboldened to walk toward Grace and gently place a hand on her elbow. "Honey, I don't know anything about it."

"I'm sure they told you," Grace huffed.

"No, sweetie."

"You mean you don't even know what got me into trouble? You don't know why you are having to do this little project?" Grace asked in disbelief. She had one hand on her hip, and she gestured in frustration with the other. Colleen was silent. "All this time, you didn't even know I like to cook?"

This was a new kind of strong reaction from Grace. She was either stunned, or she was accusing Colleen of lying to her; and Colleen didn't quite know what to make of it.

"As far as why you got into trouble, I asked Mrs. Johnson not to tell me. It didn't really matter to me."

"But, I thought that's why you were the one that volunteered to work with me, why you didn't put me off on somebody else." Grace didn't take her eyes off Colleen now, looking for a sign that she was lying. Her volume kept rising with each new thought. "You like to cook, and you knew I got in trouble for stealing that ingredient; so that's why you came up with this idea about making food for the shelter, to teach me about *thinking about other people* and *doing the right thing!*"

"Grace, sit down," Colleen said. Her tone was gentle, yet firm. It was the first time she had been authoritative with the girl, and Grace took a seat at the kitchen table obediently.

"I wanted to get to know you first. The real you. I was afraid that if they told me about this little mistake you made that it might muddy my perception. Do you understand?"

Grace nodded, believing Colleen now but still surprised.

"Do you want to tell me about it?"

Grace opened her mouth, and the words came out like long-time prisoners through broken bars. She told Colleen and Melody that she loved to cook in the children's home kitchen. Her favorite thing to watch on television had been cooking shows for as long as she could remember. She told them how great the houseparents were, always willing to help her try new things in the kitchen and supervise her so she could hone her skills. They even let her help prepare meals for the other children.

"But a few weeks ago, I really, really wanted to try out this recipe. We had most of the stuff I needed, but it called for thyme, and we didn't have any." Grace spoke faster and faster. "I went to the store with one of the housemoms, Gina, but she said we had a really tight budget for the week, and she wouldn't add it to the list. I wanted the dish to be perfect; so, I took it, just put it in my bag. It was only a three-dollar bottle of spice! It wasn't a big deal, but they said I couldn't go to the store anymore, and I got so mad! That's why I broke some stuff in the kitchen, just some stupid plates. And then they banned me from the kitchen, too. So now I can't even cook anymore, except here."

Colleen's heart ached for the girl. She could understand how one bad choice can take you down like quicksand. *That's the nature in us all,* she thought. And now, the one thing that meant the most to Grace, the way she expressed herself, was being withheld, although for just reasons. The truth was, Grace's love for cooking was the only reason she hadn't protested more about the service project from the beginning.

So much made sense to Colleen now. *That's why she hasn't been giving me a harder time,* Colleen thought. *She enjoys cooking! This was never really a punishment.* Colleen also remembered Marsha Whitefield's comment at church, about it being a treat for Grace to learn from her and cook in her kitchen.

"I bet it feels good to get that out," Melody said gently.

Grace didn't answer, but she did feel better. She worried, though, that Colleen wished she had known earlier. She wondered if Colleen would have agreed to let her even step foot in her kitchen if she had known.

Will she back out now? Grace thought. *Will she be afraid that I might start breaking dishes in her kitchen? I might not get to cook here anymore or make soap for the women's shelter.*

Grace looked at Colleen and was amazed to see the most genuine smile she had ever seen. Then Colleen started to laugh, slowly, then building to a joyful resonance.

"Honey, do you know what this means?" Colleen asked, trying to hold back more happy laughter.

Grace's mouth gaped. Colleen's reaction was surprising and strange to her.

"We didn't plan any of this based on what you did or your love for cooking, but you're *here*. Mrs. Johnson didn't know I was the one that would volunteer, but I *did*." She saw the light in Grace's eyes begin to shine. "It all works out, honey. Everything works out." Her words begged Grace to believe her. "Even Melody losing her job so she could join us. There's purpose in everything! We may not see it or understand it, but that doesn't mean it's not there."

Listening to her mother's words, Melody felt a tear come to her eye, but it didn't spill. She had the most wonderful peace, reassured of God's purpose. She came closer to Grace, who looked almost limp with relief. "God wants you here, Grace," she said, patting her knee. "And so do we."

Chapter Twenty-One

OLD DREAMS AND NEW IDEAS

SATURDAY CONVERSATIONS AT THE DINER hadn't been the same since Grace came into Colleen's life. She loved telling Harvey about the breakthroughs she saw, the ways Grace was learning, and how much they had accomplished together. He listened intently as Colleen told him about the events in the kitchen on Tuesday.

"All along, she loved to cook, and I didn't know about it!" Colleen exclaimed. "Isn't it amazing how God works things out?"

She was halfway through a bite of grits when Harvey said something that made Colleen almost choke on her breakfast.

"Have you ever thought that she might be the one? The one we always said we would adopt?"

She was certainly surprised by the question, but the truth was, she had considered it many times. The idea first occurred to Colleen after her conversation with Becky, about what would happen when the LML project was over.

Before Harvey and Colleen were ever married, they discussed the type of family they wanted. The family they envisioned included several children, some of whom would be adopted like Colleen herself had been.

Colleen's mother and father had one son in 1952, then lost a daughter at birth three years later. Six years after the loss of their daughter, their joy was restored by the addition of a three-year-old, blonde-haired, blue-eyed little girl—a girl who needed them as much as they needed her.

Colleen had always known she was adopted, but she was very fortunate not to remember a life before her adoptive family. Her childhood was marked by love and happiness in a home with a mother and father and the security of family.

Ever since she was a teenager, Colleen entertained thoughts about adopting a child—not because she had been adopted, but because it just seemed like the right thing to do.

"I know what we had planned," Colleen answered Harvey. "I just thought we waited too late. We devoted so much time to the twins, and then it never seemed like the right time. Don't you think we're getting too old?"

"Sarah was ninety," Harvey said matter-of-factly. "Maybe it's time to push that dream over the goal line."

Colleen smiled and hid her face in her hands. "Oh, Harvey," she said looking up. "I can't believe you actually brought it up."

"I just wanted to let you know I'm praying about it, just in case." Harvey may have been a man of few words, but he knew how to communicate with God.

Colleen's brain felt like a whirligig. *Could this be it?* she thought. *Could this be what I've been chasing all this time?* She didn't know for sure, but just the idea that adopting Grace might be the solution for her restless soul made Colleen feel lighter. It was an interesting possibility. Two of Colleen's favorite words were *purpose* and *possibility,* and she loved them even more when they were put together.

Being retired and having raised their kids already, she thought it shouldn't be too hard to find the time to complete all the requirements for adopting. Colleen had researched the process about a dozen times over the years, each time her desire to pursue adopting ignited and, eventually, dulled again. The many hours of classes, the home studies, the in-depth background checks—there was a lot involved to be licensed by the state.

Carrying the twins for nine months and then birthing them into the world had not been easy either, and Colleen thought of the fostering and adoption process as a similar labor of love. The requirements weren't easy, but she felt in her soul that the reward would be great.

I just want to do the right thing for Grace, though, she thought.

Colleen knew she had a lot of praying to do to find the answer.

They had walked to the diner; so, with full bellies and full hearts, Harvey and Colleen strolled back home, hand-in-hand. It was sidewalk most of the way to their bungalow-style house. There were a few neighbors out for them to stop and shake hands with as they passed or wave to from across the lawn. The weather was unseasonably comfortable for late July, so they were in no hurry to get inside.

"Where has this summer gone?" Harvey asked rhetorically. "These last few months have been a blur. Fall will be here before we know it."

"I know, honey," Colleen agreed. "And in just two more weeks, I'll have my second audition, and the fair is almost here! And you know what? There's only four more Tuesdays of Grace's service project, too. What do you think about starting the Mountain-to-Sea Trail in the fall? Not all of it. We'll just pick a stretch."

Harvey ignored the question.

"You're already halfway done with her service hours?"

It seemed the weeks clicked by faster and faster every year, and that was the only part of getting older that bothered Harvey. He didn't mind the gray hair or the spare tire. But he knew his time on earth was a finite commodity.

Having a young person in the house again might help turn back the clock a bit, Harvey thought.

As soon as they arrived home, the phone rang; and to their surprise, it was Grace.

"Hey, Colleen." Grace sounded excited. "This could have waited until Tuesday, but I wanted to ask you something about making more soap. I have some ideas!"

"Okay," Colleen answered her with equal excitement. "What's on your mind? I want to hear all about it!"

"I'd like to make some gift packs for the kids here at Oak Grove, if that's okay. And I wonder if there are any other kinds of shelters around that might like to have them. Or your nursing home?"

"That would be wonderful!" Colleen answered. We're going to have plenty, and we can always make more. You keep thinkin' of who might could use them."

"Okay," Grace said happily. "Well, here's Mrs. Johnson. She wants to talk to you. Oh, but one more thing—do you want to pick me up for church again tomorrow?"

"I'll see you in the morning."

"Okay, bye!"

Grace handed the phone to Becky.

"Hi, Colleen! That's one excited girl, isn't it?"

"She sure is! I'm so proud of her. She really does have great ideas."

"Well, we are definitely interested in having some of those soaps she keeps talking about. That was a remarkable thing to start doing with Grace. Not only does she learn the skill, but she's learning so much about philanthropy, giving of her time and energy to make other people happy. We really appreciate what you are doing."

Colleen was glad that Becky seemed so confident in their work now.

"We're getting along just fine," said Colleen. "And my daughter, Melody, is helping us out while she's in-between jobs."

"Oh, yes. That's another thing I wanted to talk with you about. Grace talks non-stop about Melody to her friends here. I think it's wonderful that she looks up to her so much!" She paused to clear her throat. "But since we don't have her on file here as a volunteer, she's going to need to submit an application."

"Oh, I hadn't thought of that!" Colleen said. "I hope it's not a problem. Grace is always with me when Melody is here, and it just didn't cross my mind."

"It's fine, Colleen. Just have her come in as soon as she can to fill out the paperwork."

"I'll call her right away," Colleen assured her. "Enjoy your day off tomorrow, and we'll be by to pick up Grace around ten-thirty."

Colleen hung up and immediately dialed Melody's number, as she had promised. Melody was halfway through a workout video in the middle of her living room and was pretty happy for the interruption.

After learning about the volunteer requirements, Melody decided it would be nice to work with Grace in a more official capacity. "I'll go down and get everything squared away on Monday," she said.

It made Melody's heart swell when her mother told her about Grace's idea to expand the distribution of *Grace & Lavender* soaps. She felt like their work was worthwhile, and she was proud of Grace. There were so many places that could benefit from something as simple as bars of soap, and it was something real and tangible they could make and give away to show love.

"How's the job search going?" Colleen asked before they hung up the phone.

"Slow," answered Melody. She was smiling. "But I'm not worried. God has a plan."

Chapter Twenty-Two

OLD FRIENDS AND NEW DREAMS

WHEN MELODY HUNG UP THE phone from her mother, she didn't go back to her workout video. Checking her watch, she realized she had to get ready for her lunch date instead.

She showered, using a brand-new bar of strong-smelling lavender soap she had made herself. She dressed quickly, then decided she didn't like the shorts and t-shirt she had picked out. She traded the outfit for a cute skirt, knit top, and a short-sleeve cardigan and examined herself in the mirror.

"There, that's better," she said. The new outfit seemed much more appropriate for meeting someone she hadn't seen in so many years.

For the last two days, she had been thinking about Jason. It was still hard to believe he had called her out of the blue. It had been so long since she'd heard his voice, at first it didn't seem real; but there was no mistaking it was him.

Jason Green grew up in the house across the street from the Hills and had been a frequent guest in their home. When she heard his familiar "Hey, Mel," it brought back a flood of memories from her childhood all at once—memories of Little League games, popsicles on the backyard swing set, hide and seek, and bicycle races. Then she thought of high school.

A year older than Melody and Michael, Jason had driven them to and from school every day for half of high school. Melody and Jason even went to the prom together as friends his senior year.

After high school, Jason joined the army and received a few paid vacations to "the Sandbox." That's why the two had lost touch. But he was back in Springville, most likely for good.

On their call, Melody learned that Jason had found a little house to rent in town and had recently started working as a deputy for the county sheriff's office.

"I can't believe you're back in Springville!" she had told him. "I imagined you'd be off seeing the world."

"No. I've seen a lot of things that made me come to really appreciate this little town. I'm glad to be right here, where it's calm and quiet most of the time. Plus, I felt like this is where God wants me to be."

Lunch was his idea, and Melody had been looking forward to their reunion ever since the phone call.

When she pulled up in front of the diner where they had planned to meet, he was standing outside waiting for her. *He hasn't changed a bit,* she thought when she first laid eyes on him. *Except for those muscles!* Army life had changed his physique quite a bit, but he still had the same sideways grin; and he still stood with his thumbs through his belt loops like he used to.

Jason met her halfway to the door. He looked thrilled to see her, but he still had the same shy and reserved manner she remembered.

They found a booth in the back of the restaurant where they could talk without too much distraction. There was so much to catch up on, and after ordering, they wasted no time learning about the years they had lost.

When Melody asked questions about his time on active duty, he shied away from some of them. But he talked freely about the friends he had made and some of the sites he had visited. She was amazed at the things he had seen and done in his time away from Springville.

He asked her about college and what she liked to do for fun now. She answered; then she told him about the job she had just lost and about her apartment. She talked about her niece and how cute she was. She even talked in-depth about her new soap-making hobby, and he listened as if it were the most interesting subject in the world. Their exchange was so easy and carefree, and an hour passed like only ten minutes. By the time they had finished their sandwiches and moved on to pie, it seemed like they had never been apart.

"How are your parents doing now?" Melody asked. She ran into Mr. and Mrs. Green from time-to-time in Springville, and she always asked them about Jason; but it had been a while since she'd seen them.

"Oh, they're great! Staying busy!" he said. He told Melody about their real estate ventures and, specifically, about the commercial property they owned downtown. "They're looking for small businesses to move in right now," he told her. "Apparently, there's all this grant money for a downtown revitalization project. Downtown has been dead for so long. The right business could open shop and get it rent-free for the first year. It's pretty incredible."

He took a big bite of pecan pie, while Melody agreed that it was incredible. She had never heard of a program like that, and she thought it would be wonderful to see the downtown area brought back to life.

"Hey! Maybe you should open a boutique and sell your homemade soap!" Jason said, still chewing. At first, Melody scoffed at the idea, but Jason was persistent. "Trust me. Life is short. If this is something you enjoy doing, you should go after it hard. I think my parents are checking on properties today. They could probably meet us down there right now."

Renting a retail space on Main Street in Springville was not something Melody had ever dreamed of doing. But she was starting to learn that life could be as unpredictable as a toddler without a nap.

It was a far cry from human resources specialist, but as they talked it over, she started to think there might actually be a market for handmade soaps and soap-making classes in Springville. People appreciated hand-crafted things, and buying local had become trendy.

When he saw a glimmer of excitement in Melody's eyes, Jason was determined to help make it happen, and all it took was one phone call.

Mr. and Mrs. Green were gracious to meet with her and walk her through the space with little notice. They had always liked Melody, and years ago, they had secretly wished she and Jason would start dating.

Melody was in a whirlwind, seeing Jason after so long and entertaining such a bold move in the same day. But when she walked through the quaint, empty store, she had an overwhelming peace. She almost laughed, wondering how on earth she wound up there; then she felt the attitude of her mother being born in her. *I just feel like I need to do this. I need to do this.*

She had enough severance pay to invest in getting a little business up and running, although it would be a modest start. She worked out the details of the rental agreement with Mr. and Mrs. Green that very afternoon, with her old friend by her side the entire time.

Melody, the young woman so concerned about her own lack of ambition just a few weeks before, jumped headfirst into a business venture, with little capital and no business plan, but with a whisper of approval from Heaven.

Chapter Twenty-Three

DISTRACTIONS

THE SUNDAY MORNING SERVICE WAS both uplifting and chal-
lenging. Pastor Daniel T. Whitefield had a little more fire in his
voice than normal as he preached on the concept of reaping and
sowing. Sunshine came through the stained-glass windows in a
straight beam to the pulpit, creating a spotlight on the preacher's
perspiring forehead. Cardboard fans flapped in synchronous motion
throughout the congregation.

Grace, in her same navy dress, sat close to Colleen on the pew. She
kept her eyes focused on the preacher and seemed to hang on every
word. Colleen, however, didn't give the pastor's passionate oration the
attention it deserved. Her mind started chasing rabbits mid-sermon
because the subject of reaping and sowing made her think of *Risk
and Reward*. It wasn't quite the same thing; but once her brain made
the connection, she became wrapped up in game show dreams, and
Pastor Whitefield started to look a whole lot like Rodney Vaughn. To
Colleen's ears only, he even started to sound like him, too. And when
he asked the congregation what they could be doing to serve the Lord
better, Colleen almost slapped her Bible like a buzzer. Harvey felt her
fidgeting on the pew beside him and instinctively shot her the same
settle down look he used to give the twins.

When church was over, Colleen felt remorse for having let herself get so distracted; but she was meeting the producers of *Risk and Reward* in less than two weeks, and her excitement was getting hard to contain. One meeting could change her entire life. It could mean a national television appearance! *I'll pay more attention next week,* she told herself.

Colleen wasn't the only one in the family distracted by excitement and big possibilities that morning. Melody could hardly believe she had made a major life decision without telling her parents first. *Daddy is going to think I've gone crazy,* she thought, genuinely worried, but also amused at her own hutzpah. *This is something that Mama would do, but not me!* Her right hand gripped her left one so tightly, she'd made them both sore without realizing it.

Melody sat on a pew very similar to the one on which her parents and Grace sat, but in the small church within walking distance of her apartment. She prayed and hoped with all her heart that she had made a good decision; and she prayed that if she hadn't, God would bless her new venture anyway.

What do I have to lose? she thought as she reflected on the lightning-fast events.

While the choir sang, Melody thought about shelving units and product displays, pricing and promotion, supply and demand, inventory and ingredients. *I hope the reward outweighs the risk,* she thought.

The following day, the scales of emotion had tipped, and the excitement outweighed the concern. The motivation was there from the moment she woke up, accompanied by a beautiful peace. Melody was eager to get started, feeling like this new day was the beginning of an important chapter in her life.

As soon as the administrative office of Oak Grove Children's Home was open, she was there to complete the volunteer application. She was interested to see where Grace lived. She felt so close to the child, but really knew little about her life. On the way in, she surveyed the home and its tile floors and long, stark hallways. It looked very clean, and the smell of bleach invaded her nostrils. Melody envisioned Grace walking down the hallway, trying to imagine for a moment what it must be like for her and the other children there day-to-day.

Melody spent more time with Becky Johnson than she had planned, but it was an important visit.

"Normally, our volunteer coordinator handles all the screenings and applications," Becky said, "but Grace is a special case to me. I like to be involved in all issues that concern her." Becky's voice was wistful. "I pray every day that God will put the right people in Grace's life, and it seems that He is doing just that."

By the time she left, Melody had learned a lot about Grace and more about the children's home and about being a volunteer. Becky was warm and engaging, and Melody enjoyed talking with her. Some stories she heard, though, made her cry, right there in front of Becky—stories about children discarded like yesterday's newspaper or who found themselves playing second fiddle to mama and daddy's next fix.

The conversations with Becky lingered in Melody's mind for a long time, and she was still feeling emotional, even as she began to tackle the job of cleaning up the store. But she threw herself into the work of scrubbing and shining the floors, walls, and counters, then stood back when she was finished and admired the empty store like a proud parent with a new baby. Never had an empty room seemed so full. She sat down cross-legged right on the floor, overwhelmed by what she had done, overwhelmed by the place and time in which she had found herself so quickly. Two words formulated in her brain as she stared at the space, and she saw them written in giant, animated letters, bouncing off the walls and ceiling and floor in a continuous motion: *purpose, possibilities, purpose, possibilities, purpose, possibilities . . . purpose.*

The space had previously been a high-end coffee shop, which hadn't gone over well in Springville. But it meant that the little store already had a kitchen for making soaps and a perfect-size main room for selling them. She closed her eyes and envisioned what it could be. She could even smell the lavender as she pictured shoppers headed out the door, loaded down with cute little shopping bags filled with her soaps . . . *their* soaps.

Although she knew little about business, Melody had researched the craft of soap-making over the last few weeks as if she were cramming for final exams in college. She knew where to buy supplies in bulk. She knew the different methods to produce different results. She knew it would take a long time to perfect her craft; but the soap she had made so far was of excellent quality, and she was proud of her product.

Never a very crafty or creative person before, it was amazing how the hobby had taken hold of her. There was just so much about it that she loved—the smell, the process, the decorative packaging, the look of the final product. She had tried many recipes and processes, in both her mother's kitchen and at her own apartment. She loved the refreshing feeling of bathing with her own creations. The bars left her skin feeling soft, and the smells were fresh and relaxing.

Melody couldn't wait to surprise her family with her wild plan. Her parents had always encouraged her to pursue her dreams, so she was certain they would be just as excited about the store as she was. But when Melody closed her eyes and imagined showing off the space, what she pictured was the look on Grace's face.

I want her to like it here, she thought. *I want her to feel at home here.*

Chapter Twenty-Four
THE BIG SURPRISE

"I'VE NEVER MADE LASAGNA BEFORE," Grace said. "It's easier than I thought it would be."

"Well, cooking comes more naturally to some than others. It's one of your gifts," Colleen replied as she rinsed utensils in the sink.

"My gifts?" Grace sounded as if she had just heard a happy surprise.

"Yes! Just look at how perfectly you sliced those tomatoes for the salad. You think everybody can do that?"

Grace looked at her handiwork and smiled. Now that her secret was out, and she didn't have to hide how much she loved being in the kitchen, she worked with pride and purpose.

With preparations finished, Grace and Colleen sat at the kitchen table, flipping through the cookbook that had Colleen's face on the cover.

"I want you to plan the meal for next week," Colleen said. "Is there anything special you want to learn how to cook?"

Grace's dark eyes lit up, and she looked stunned. "Plan the whole meal by myself? That would be awesome!"

"Sure! You know enough about cooking to plan a great meal. Just make it something that's easy to make a lot of at one time, and keep the ingredients economical. The Ladies' Ministry League might not have the budget for steak."

Colleen got up from the table and retrieved a notepad and pen from the what-not drawer. "Here you go," she said, handing them to Grace. "You decide what we're gonna make and write down all the ingredients we'll need, while I finish cleaning up."

"Okay!" Grace dove into the recipes, searching for just the right one. She already had a few ideas.

Colleen dipped her hands in the dishwater and began scrubbing a pan. "I can't wait to find out what Melody's surprise is! It must be something important for her to miss soap-making day."

"I miss her," Grace said, flipping pages.

Colleen loved the way Grace had taken to Melody. *They would make good sisters,* she thought. *But it's way too early to be thinking about that. I need to keep praying about it and give it some time.*

With regard to Grace, Colleen had to fight her impulsive nature. She understood she couldn't treat adopting a child as a project, like making soap or writing a cookbook.

"Well, we'll see her soon and find out what she's up to," Colleen assured her.

Curiosity had overwhelmed Colleen all day, ever since Melody called early that morning with unusual instructions.

"Mama, everything's fine," she had said, "but I can't come over to make soap with Grace today. I have something to show you and Daddy, though, and I want you to bring Grace, too."

Colleen was dumbfounded, but excited. "She sounded so happy!" she told Harvey, as she explained the phone call. "She wants us to deliver the food early and meet her downtown."

"Downtown?" Harvey had questioned. "What could possibly be going on downtown?" Both parents were mystified.

Between the pending reveal of Melody's surprise, waiting on the confirmation of her game show ambition, and entertaining the possibility of parenting a teenager again, Colleen was almost maxed out on excitement. Her goal to make life interesting was being met in a big way, even causing *her* restless heart to settle down a bit. At least Tuesdays with Grace were normal and comfortable now. The only stress was that there were just two more of them scheduled, and Colleen didn't know where they would go from there.

The oven timer sounded to let Colleen and Grace know the pans of pasta were finished baking. "Ooh, let me get them!" Grace said, jumping up from the table and grabbing the oven mitts.

Soon, the meal was packed up; and Colleen, Harvey, and Grace delivered it to the women and children at the shelter in plenty of time to meet Melody before Grace was due back at Oak Grove.

"Now *where* am I supposed to meet her?" Harvey asked as he turned onto Main Street.

"She said she would be at the Soda Shop at four o'clock," Colleen reminded him.

The Soda Shop was one of the last businesses remaining downtown. It was such an iconic place, such a part of Springville's history, people still went out of their way to stop in for a hot dog from time-to-time.

"There she is!" Grace said, as Harvey pulled the SUV up to the curb. Melody was standing out front, waving with both hands like she was meeting celebrities instead of her parents and Grace. She wore cuffed denim shorts and a zipped-up jacket, despite the heat.

Grace got out of the car and bounded over to her; then she took a step back, not sure how the greeting should go. Melody assisted by offering a high-five and a big smile. "I'm so glad you're here, Grace!"

Melody's parents each greeted her with a hug, and they both looked around to see if the big surprise was nearby and obvious.

"You've got us all in suspense, baby girl!" Colleen said, patting her daughter on the back.

The street was quiet, and there were few people in the restaurant and store behind them. Melody stood there with just her parents and Grace as an audience, beaming as if the whole world was hers. "Okay!" she said, taking a deep breath to inflate her confidence. "Follow me."

She led them straight across the street to a brick building, to the middle store in a row of three vacant shops. A large window revealed that the space was empty, so there appeared to be no surprise waiting on the sidewalk out front or inside. There was no signage, no shingle, no indication of any value there, until Melody took a key from her pocket and placed it in the lock on the front door.

"What is this place?" her daddy asked as Melody led them all inside. Colleen was too intrigued to speak. She looked around, then at Melody, then around the room again.

Melody took another deep, bracing breath. "This is my store," she said. "Or you might call it . . . our store." She gestured toward all of them.

"A store for what?" The quiet one was the only one asking the questions.

Melody led them toward the back, revealing the kitchen around a corner. "For making and selling soap," she said, gesturing toward both parts of the space. "*Grace & Lavender* soaps." She ceremoniously unzipped her unseasonable jacket to reveal a t-shirt underneath. The *Grace & Lavender* logo was printed on the front.

Grace's mouth dropped open, and Colleen's mouth finally clamped shut as she understood the possibilities. Her eyes locked with her daughter's, and Melody read that she was already onboard.

"Grace, are you going to be okay with your name being used? The name you came up with for our soap?" Melody asked. "I probably should have asked you first, but I really want the store to be called *Grace & Lavender*. It has so much meaning."

Grace nodded her head emphatically up and down.

"Okay," said Harvey, "slow down. Tell us how this happened!"

Grace cared, but wasn't overly interested in how it happened. She was interested in what it really meant and how she might get to be a part of it. Melody told her parents all about lunch with Jason, and about his parents' real estate business, and about the grant money. She tried to help them understand why she had jumped so quickly into unknown territory, while Grace surveyed the front room.

The white tile floor was spotless. The window in front gleamed as if to say *look at me* to passing shoppers, had there been any. The interior walls were bricked, just like the outside. The paneled ceiling held rows of long, fluorescent tube bulbs that hadn't been turned on in months. The power wouldn't be cut back on until the next day, so all Melody's cleaning had been done in the late summer heat with no air conditioning. The store was still dead, but the scrubbing it had received was the first step in its resurrection.

Colleen wore a smile a mile wide. She stood peering into the kitchen while Melody kept talking, hardly stopping to take a breath. Colleen could already envision the micro-factory in action.

"Sweetie, you know we'll help you any way we can," Harvey said. "If this makes you happy, then I'm all for it."

Melody wrapped her arms around her father's big barrel chest, leaning her head against him. "Thank you, Daddy!"

She looked at her mother and at Grace, waiting on them to say something.

"Are you really going to turn this place into a store for our soaps? Like, a real store?" Grace asked, running her hand down the long, wooden counter that was the only fixture in the front room.

"I'm going to try," Melody answered. "And I hope you'll be able to help me! I've already talked to Mrs. Johnson, and she said we would try to work something out."

It caught Colleen off-guard that Melody had talked to Becky about Grace without her knowing it. It made her feel strange; but she couldn't quite pinpoint the emotion, so she shook it off.

Melody turned to her parents. "I know I may not be able to support myself financially by doing this. I haven't completely lost my mind. But I want to try it for a while. And I'll take as much help with the work as you want to give."

Colleen looked at Harvey, then back to Melody, and smiled. "When do we get started?" she asked. "You know I love a challenge!"

Chapter Twenty-Five
PROGRESS

"I'M SO GLAD MRS. JOHNSON let you work with me today, Grace," Melody said. "This really is a big help."

The goal of the day was inventory. A store couldn't run without something to sell, and they were starting from relatively little stock.

Melody had invested in new molds and new oils and a variety of other different ingredients in bulk, and large cooling racks had been delivered the day before. It wasn't just about lavender anymore, although Melody was keeping *Grace & Lavender* as the name of the store and the brand. Now they were making soap with chamomile, honey, lemongrass, oatmeal, coffee, and other natural ingredients. The place smelled amazing.

Making soap was so similar to cooking—the measuring, pouring, and mixing, along with the wonderful smells—that Grace naturally enjoyed it.

Melody was glad the kitchen had a window, so they were able to ventilate when they mixed the lye. They made sure to use goggles and gloves as well.

"I feel like a scientist in a lab!" Grace chuckled. Melody took out her phone to snap a picture of Grace in all her gear, stirring the pot.

Melody taught Grace about the chemical reaction between the fats in the oils and the lye, and she couldn't stop laughing when Grace started saying the scientific term for the reaction over and over, just because she thought it was fun to say.

"Saponification. Saponification. Saponification."

After the first batch had cooked long enough, the pair worked together to pour the pudding-like substance into special honeycomb-patterned molds. Melody held the pot while Grace used a wooden spoon to guide the young soap where it needed to be. Three other batches still cooked on the stovetop.

Although it wasn't necessary, Melody thought it was better to let the soap cure for a couple of weeks before selling it, so it was important to start on production right away. While the inventory cured, Melody would have plenty of time to set up the store and to do some advertising, too.

She had plans to sell to other stores and at farmer's markets, and she would even start an online store. She wanted to run a promotion on a new product each week, and she planned to give out free samples to encourage people to try different scents. One of Melody's favorite ideas was to teach classes in the store's kitchen once a month, to help people learn how to make their own homemade soaps.

The ideas to make her business work were clicking away in her brain almost faster than she could process them, and she knew they had to be from the Lord. The whole thing seemed to have a Divine purpose. She realized some might think something as ordinary as a soap store couldn't possibly be part of a heavenly agenda, but Melody knew differently.

Colleen was at home for the day, caring for Prairie; so for the first time, Melody and Grace worked together alone. Melody was thankful for the opportunity to get to know Grace in her own way. Grace was so pleasant, so excited to be there and to be helping. She felt ownership of the process, and she took pride in what they were doing.

"I think we should donate at least ten percent of everything we make," Melody announced. "And . . . I think you should be our charitable donations coordinator."

Melody put a hand on her hip and looked at Grace to see her reaction. She was beaming.

"I know you have some great ideas, like giving to the children's home and the nursing home. Make a list of all your ideas; then we can look over it together and figure out how we want to make them happen."

"Okay!"

"I think if you help me plan and deliver the soap we're donating, that might even count toward your service hours."

Grace's brow furrowed, and she looked away from Melody.

"What's wrong?" Melody asked.

"Well, it's just that . . . I love being here and making soap with you, but I love cooking with your mom, too, and . . . " Grace hesitated.

"Go ahead, it's okay . . . "

"Well, I don't have many hours left of the project, of my *punishment,* and I don't want to have to choose how I spend them."

Melody saw the effort it had taken for Grace to open up, to be straight with her. And she felt like Grace deserved the same. She and her mother had both been so careful with the girl. They knew she was fragile. They knew she had been hurt, and they didn't want to risk hurting her more. They had been treating her like an injured kitten. But she was fourteen, and Melody felt it was time to be more direct.

"Grace, listen," she said. "I don't know exactly what's going to happen after this project with you and my mom and the Ladies' Ministry League is over. But I like spending time with you. And you helped inspire my crazy idea to start this store. *Grace & Lavender* is partly yours."

Grace looked down, but her pride was obvious.

"You don't have to choose. I know my mom loves cooking with you, too. She likes having you around. And I've seen how great you are in the kitchen. I think you have a real future as a chef, if that's what you want to do someday. You should keep honing your skills whenever you can."

Future. Grace's brain stumbled on the word. She rarely thought about it. Sometimes, she struggled to remember her past, and it made the future seem inconsequential. She mostly focused on the now and just getting through each day. That was much easier than confronting the uncertainty that she was sure to face down the road, when she was no longer in the care of the state.

Melody went on. "I can't tell you how things will go. I can't promise that we'll see each other every week. But the end of the project doesn't have to be the end of seeing you. We'll try our best to make sure of that." She wanted to say so much more, to tell Grace just how much she wanted to be part of her life. But it wasn't the time.

Grace looked her in the eye, nodded, and said, "Okay." The four-letter word carried a lot of weight. She hadn't let her ears tune out the sincerity of Melody's words. She hadn't scoffed at them. She was choosing to believe them. She was choosing to trust someone. And that moment was worth the entire day's work.

Melody had found the last two keys to unlocking the door to Grace's heart. Along with love and patience, it was honesty and commitment that she needed, and Melody had shown her both.

By the end of the day, there were twelve dozen molded bars of soap cooling on the tall metal racks in the front room of the store. But they had made progress in more ways than one.

Chapter Twenty-Six

A HOME LIKE THIS

MELODY WAS GRATEFUL TO HAVE a calm, Sunday lunch with just her mother and father. After such hard work and excitement, she could think of nothing better than relaxing in their company, enjoying her mother's cooking, and just being back home for a while.

As she made her way up the front walk, she studied the house thoughtfully. It was a place she loved with all her being. It was a peaceful, inviting home, and it was a part of who she was.

The *welcome* mat on the porch of her parents' house was the same one that had been there for years. Its message was intended to be taken literally, and most people in town knew it.

Her father kept the shrubs neatly trimmed and the area around them free of weeds. All the bushes were evergreen, so the front of the house always looked the same every time she came.

Melody imagined herself as a little girl, writing with chalk on the walkway; as a pre-teen, turning cartwheels in the yard; and as a teenager, sitting on the porch swing with friends. She had changed, but the house had not; and she knew this was still her home, no matter how old she was and no matter where she laid down to rest at night. It was a feeling of security, knowing she always had a place to go.

How is it that I was blessed with a home like this, and so many others were not? I wish everyone could have this. Her thought was a subconscious prayer.

She walked through the front doorway of her childhood home. She didn't have to knock or ring the doorbell. She smelled the familiar smells of her mother's famous chicken pie, and it brought a smile to her face.

"Oh, Mama!" Melody exclaimed during lunch, talking with food in her mouth like a little kid. "This is so delicious. Just taking a few bites has me feeling rejuvenated already!"

Melody finally knew what people meant when they talked about a *good* kind of tired. It wasn't that she had ever been a slothful person. She had just never known what it was like to put so much effort into a goal and watch it materialize.

"I'm glad you like it, honey," her mother said. "By the way, your brother wants to come see the store. You should call him. Oh! And I forgot to tell you! Prairie asked for her Aunt Mel on Friday!"

"I need to go see her soon," Melody said. "I miss the little munchkin."

They talked a little about the store and her progress. Melody and Harvey discussed plans for him to come over on Monday to assemble some shelving units. Colleen offered to come by Thursday after the LML meeting to help make more soap and package the soap that had already set.

Melody sat there long after she finished her second helping, just enjoying the conversation. She felt filled to the brim with love and chicken pie.

She told her parents how well it had gone with Grace on Friday. "I think she really had fun helping me," Melody said. "And Jason came by yesterday to see what I was doing at the store."

"Oh, he did, did he?" Harvey pretended to be worried about his baby girl entertaining a male guest.

"Yes, Daddy," Melody said. "And he even helped make some soap."

Colleen and Harvey were both thrilled that Melody and Jason's friendship had been revived.

"Is there anything else going on with you that we should know about?" her mother asked.

"Yeah, well, they're raising the rent on my apartment again next month." Melody rolled her eyes, wishing she had good news to report instead.

"Maybe you should look for a different place?" her father suggested. "Rent is much cheaper in Springville."

"Or you might even be able to find a house you can afford!" her mother encouraged.

"It's probably not a good time to buy right now. I may need to wait until I find a *real* job again," Melody said with a chuckle.

The conversation shifted to *Risk and Reward* and the meeting on Wednesday. "Don't get her started," Harvey warned Melody. "She's already like a kernel of corn in hot oil."

Colleen had her charming stories all planned out. She also thought aloud about taking a can of preserves and some homemade soap to give to the producers, but she decided she might be disqualified for bribery.

The conversation started to lull as brains caught up with stomachs, and they realized how full they all were. Melody felt like if she didn't get up, she might not be able to in a few minutes.

"I'll clear the table," she said, rising reluctantly from her chair.

"Hold on, honey," Colleen said, motioning for her to sit back down. She gave Harvey a look that was a silent question. He nodded affirmatively.

"We want to talk to you about something else. Just an idea right now," Colleen said. "But we thought we should go ahead and mention it."

"What is it?" Melody asked. "It sounds important."

"It is important," Harvey said in a tone that reassured Melody that it was a happy idea, and that nothing was wrong.

"Go ahead! Tell me!"

"Well," said Colleen, "We've been thinking about adopting another child."

Colleen said *another* as if Melody and Michael still lived with her, instead of away on their own.

"Not just any child," Colleen added before Melody had time to ask questions. "We think we might want to adopt Grace. What do you think about that?" Colleen looked at Melody with joy on her face, hoping to see the emotion reciprocated. It wasn't.

"You can't do that," Melody said in a firm, even tone.

Colleen and Harvey looked at each other, shocked by their daughter's directness.

"Well, honey, what do you mean?" her mother asked.

"I mean you can't adopt Grace . . . because I'm going to." Melody was staunch, and almost defensive, but mostly confident.

Colleen's words eluded her, and her brain was too stunned to seek them out.

"Sweetie, we had no idea you felt this way. You really want to be a mother to Grace? To take care of her all by yourself?" Harvey asked.

"Yes."

It was a single word spoken with the conviction of a thousand sermons.

Colleen found words again, but sooner than she should have.

"Melody, honey, what about finding a husband and having kids of your own? Don't you think it will be harder to do that with a teenager already in your life?"

"Mother . . . " Melody started. She usually called Colleen *Mother* when she was upset, but her tone was not angry. "Aren't you always talking about living with purpose? I think she is my purpose! This is what I'm supposed to do now. And if God wants me to have a husband and more kids later, He'll give them to me."

"But, it's so sudden! How long have you thought about this?"

"Mama, what's your favorite verse of Scripture?" Melody asked, already knowing the answer.

"Proverbs, chapter three, verse six. 'In all your ways acknowledge Him, and He shall direct your paths,'" Colleen recited.

"I'm on the right path, Mama. I'm sure of it. I've already signed up for classes to become licensed as a foster parent. They start at Oak Grove next week. The way all this is working out—with Grace, with the store—it's not like me at all! That's how I know it's Him!"

"You're a very wise woman, Melody." Harvey stood up from his chair and came around the table, putting an arm around his daughter's shoulder.

Just like he had been with her sudden idea to start a business, he was behind her. She searched her mother's face to find out what she was feeling. Melody could tell that the idea of her parents adopting Grace wasn't just a whim to them; it wasn't just an item on Colleen's *Ways to Be More Interesting* checklist.

"Mama, I don't want to hurt you. Are you upset with me? Will you be okay with this?"

Colleen *was* hurt, but she was also happy because she knew that, although she hadn't seen it coming, this bend in the path was the right way to go. Soon, the happy emotion found its way to her face, and Colleen looked at her daughter with as much love as the first time she saw her.

"My Melody," Colleen said, "you've been the song of my heart since the day you were born. I could never be upset with you for pursuing God's plan for your life. And I could never begrudge you for having something I wanted."

Colleen reached past the empty mashed potato bowl and took Melody's hands. "Your happiness is most important to me."

Chapter Twenty-Seven
COULD IT BE?

COLLEEN RUMMAGED THROUGH HER CLOSET for over thirty minutes before finding an outfit to wear to her meeting with the producers.

I wonder if they provide a wardrobe for the taping of the show, she thought. *Picking out an outfit for television will be too much pressure!*

She decided on a pair of dressy, white capris and a white and hot pink flowered top with a hot pink, three-quarter-length sleeved blazer. She laid out a long, double-strand necklace with matching earrings and white pumps with the clothes.

Losing herself in excitement, Colleen broke into a jig, as she was prone to do. Her excitement was like electricity that shocked her arms, legs, and hips into spontaneous, coordinated motion.

She had called Melody three times to confirm that she was picking her up to head for Raleigh at 8:00 a.m. the next day.

"Yes, Mama, I'll be there at eight o'clock on the dot," she patiently assured each time.

I can't believe it's finally here! One more step and then I'm practically on my way to Los Angeles for taping! I'm going to be on television!

Coincidentally, a representative of the game show called in the middle of her jig.

"Hi, Mrs. Hill," the representative said after introducing himself. "I'm just calling to confirm your appointment with our production team tomorrow. We're planning on seeing you at ten-thirty. Is that still good for you?"

"Oh, absolutely! I'll be there." Colleen was a little winded from her dance.

"Great. Just relax, and be yourself during the interview. If you have any unique talents or hobbies, the team will be interested in hearing about those. Think about an anecdote that you want to share that would be good for television, something that will make you stand out."

"Oh, I can do that. I've got all kinds of stories."

"Sounds good, Mrs. Hill. Your interview will last about ten minutes. Please be sure to bring your ID with you. We look forward to seeing you tomorrow!"

What a nice young man, Colleen thought when she hung up the phone.

She was still dancing on cloud nine when Grace arrived for their Tuesday work session.

Grace had planned a dinner of beef stroganoff, and she was excited to start. As the noodles boiled and the beef cooked, Grace engaged Colleen with all types of questions about her meeting on Wednesday.

"What do you think they'll ask you? Do you think you'll find out a date for the show? Are you nervous?"

Colleen couldn't remember when she had enjoyed cooking a meal more. Grace was so pleasant, even affectionate. And she was a fantastic chef, cooking almost the entire meal on her own without guidance.

But unpredictability was becoming a theme in the lives of the Hill women, and the pleasantness with Grace wouldn't last all day.

When they delivered the food to the shelter, they saw some new families taking refuge there. Over the last few weeks, they had noticed that some women and children had moved on, hopefully to better things, and others had taken their place. They made sure to have care packages of soap ready to hand out for the life-weary newcomers.

When Grace handed a package to one of the ladies whom she had not seen there before, she found herself inexplicably shaken. There was something about the woman that disturbed her, unnerved her. She had high cheek bones and dark eyes, reminding Grace of a picture in her book on the Cherokee.

That's what it is, Grace thought. *She made me think of Mr. Hartman. That's what's wrong with me.* Grace still struggled with the thought of such a good soul being gone.

But it was something more than that. The woman walked away, and Grace watched intently as she went to get a plate of food. Her shape, the way she walked, the way she smoothed her hair down with her hands—it all seemed so familiar.

I know it's not her, Grace insisted to herself. *It's not! I haven't seen my mother in eight years, but I know that's not her. I would know my own mother, wouldn't I? Wouldn't I? And wouldn't she know me? Maybe it's a cousin. Or even a sister. I don't know.*

She noticed her breaths were coming faster and faster; and just before she spiraled into hysteria, Grace forced herself to take shelter in a bathroom. She splashed cold water on her face to shock away the notion that she might have just come face-to-face with an important piece of her past.

It took a while, but once she thought she had steeled herself enough to leave the sanctuary of the bathroom, Grace headed back out to find Colleen. She wanted to tell her what happened, but she didn't know how to explain it; and she still wasn't comfortable sharing such vulnerable emotions.

As soon as she walked into the kitchen, Colleen knew something was wrong. Grace's face was white, and her hands were shaking.

"Baby girl, what happened? Are you okay? Come over here and sit down, baby."

Colleen regularly referred to Grace as *honey*, but it was the first time she had used *baby* as a term of endearment; and the new moniker suddenly amplified the pain Grace was feeling. She knew it was just Colleen's way and that most people found it pleasant. She knew Colleen used the name with grocery store cashiers, the bank teller, and family and friends alike. But to hear it directed at her now, in this time of confusion, was more than she could handle.

She sat down in a chair, still shaking. But before Colleen could place a hand on her petite shoulder, the child sprang up in a fury.

"I'm fourteen years old! I'm too old to be someone's baby!" She glared at Colleen with a fierceness. "And you're too old to be my mother!"

The words came out of Grace's mouth before she even realized what she was saying, and they cut her almost as much as they cut Colleen. She had grown to love the woman, but the hurt in her heart still overtook love when it came time for a wrestling match.

"Okay," Colleen said, surprised by her own calmness after the emotional blow. "I know you're not a baby. But you're my friend, aren't you?" Colleen tried to step lightly, realizing that something had happened to Grace to push her outside the bounds of rationalism.

"I don't know how to be a friend!" Grace said. "Everyone I ever loved walked out on me." It was almost as if Grace was admitting that fact to herself for the first time. "Well, I guess I loved them. I can hardly remember them."

Grace sat back down, leaning over and slumping her shoulders in a defeated pose. "Some days, I don't even know how to feel anything!" she yelled into the palms of her hands.

She paused, and Colleen thought the tirade was over. But Grace had only stopped to reload. She wasn't going to allow herself to be weak.

She jumped to her feet. "And I'm tired of trying to make myself feel something that's impossible for me to feel. Don't you get it? I'm broken!" she screamed, some of the words flying out through gritted teeth. Grace's voice was hot. There were no tears. "I'm sick of all this do-gooder stuff. Like a bar of soap is actually going to make anybody feel better about their crappy life. I'm tired of all the sunshine and roses nonsense and your happy, perfect family; and I'm tired of you!"

For about as long as it took for Colleen to choke back tears, Grace stood there, wondering what move to make next. Then she ran out of the kitchen. Colleen gave chase, but she only caught a glimpse of Grace exiting the building.

Chapter Twenty-Eight
I ONCE WAS LOST . . .

I'VE NEVER SEEN COLLIE THIS upset, Harvey thought.

He sat next to her on the sofa with his rough, giant hands clasping her trembling ones. They had been sitting in the same spot for so long, his back ached, but he stayed there anyway. He was afraid if he wasn't there to prop her up, Colleen might actually collapse. Normally so strong, so confident, so optimistic, the events of the day had reduced her to a frantic, sobbing mess, and Harvey felt desperate to help her.

"Drink some more tea, honey," he said. "Maybe it will help calm you."

She didn't answer. Instead, she repeated the same story she had been reciting all night—to the sheriff's deputies, to Becky, to Melody, and over and over to Harvey.

"She just ran out the door. I tried to chase after her . . . "

"I know, honey."

" . . . but by the time I got outside, I couldn't spot her. I don't know which way she went!"

"Collie, you did your best."

"I got in the car to try to find her, but I didn't see her anywhere. I called 911."

"That's all you could do."

"I wanted to go look for her, but the deputies said to let them handle it."

"They'll find her, Collie. She's going to be okay."

Colleen was thankful that she had gotten to tell Becky herself, rather than have her hear it from the authorities. While Becky didn't accuse Colleen of any wrong doing in letting Grace run away, neither did she offer absolution like Harvey did. She was only concerned with finding Grace, and she grilled Colleen for any clues as to where Grace had gone, just like the deputies had done. Colleen regretted she had no clues to offer them.

"Becky, let me come with you to look for her," Colleen had cried into the telephone.

"No, Mrs. Hill. This concerns Oak Grove Children's Home and the sheriff's office now. I'll let you know if I hear anything."

Becky hadn't meant to be cold, but she was hurting just like Colleen.

The only comfort Colleen had was that Becky and the authorities weren't her only connection to the search for Grace. Melody had been in her car for hours, driving all over Springville. She went downtown, hoping that Grace had come to look for her at the store, but there was no sign of her. She had driven to every place she could think of that a young person might run when they wanted to get away from the world.

By midnight, she was getting discouraged, and she was scared. *Lord, please don't let anything bad happen to her,* she had prayed. *I love her.*

When a glimmer of hope surfaced, Melody called her mother to report in as she had promised to do.

The ringing of the phone made Colleen jump from the sofa. "Have you heard anything?" she practically yelled into the phone.

"Mama, calm down. I haven't seen her, and I don't know much; but I do have some news." Melody spoke very slowly and intentionally as to not excite her mother further. "I called Jason. He's not on patrol tonight, but he heard over the scanner that she may have been spotted hitchhiking on the old highway."

Colleen was both relieved that she had at least been seen and terrified at the thought of Grace traveling with strangers.

"Do you want me to come look with you?" Colleen asked, pleading.

"Mama, there's at least three patrol cars out there looking for her, plus me and Becky. And the Amber Alert went out a couple hours ago. Just stay there and pray. Pray as hard as you can."

Colleen had the presence of mind early on to call Pastor Whitefield, and he had called all the deacons of the church to ask them to pray for Grace to be found safe. Marsha had called most of the members of the LML, so they were in prayer, too. But Colleen had yet to offer up a single prayer, and she was ashamed.

All her life, Colleen had considered herself a person of faith. She had prayed in times of sickness and in times of financial trouble, and she was always faithful to give thanks for the results. But now, she couldn't manage to do anything, except blame herself and worry.

After she hung up, she made her way on shaky legs to the kitchen. She remembered how excited Grace had been, cooking the meal she had planned out herself. She remembered the first time they had cooked there together several weeks before, when the girl had hardly said a word to her. *I thought she was coming around,* thought Colleen. *I thought I was making a difference. What made her do this?*

She walked to the middle of the kitchen, between the refrigerator and the sink, and got down on her knees on the tile floor. At first, she felt that her words were bouncing off the ceiling and falling back down all around her. She lowered her face to the floor and continued to make her request anyway, her faith building with each spoken sentence. It wasn't long before peace showed up; and when it did, Colleen jumped to her feet and rushed to the phone to call Melody.

"I think I know where she is!" she said.

Chapter Twenty-Nine

. . . BUT NOW I'M FOUND

MELODY, COLLEEN, AND HARVEY RACED down country roads, with Melody at the wheel. A bright, full moon helped light the way.

Melody had been near her parents' house when she got the call, so she relented when Colleen pleaded for her to come get her. "I have to see her!" Colleen had said.

The deputies were only a short distance behind. Colleen had called from the car to let them know where they were headed to look for Grace. She just hoped the feeling she had would pan out.

They turned onto the gravel drive, and the headlights shined straight on the front of Mr. Hartman's house. Colleen immediately saw that her prayer was answered. Grace was there, laying curled up in a ball on the narrow porch.

Faster than she had moved in years, Colleen sprang from the car before Melody put it in park. The last time she had moved like that was when Melody and Michael were ten years old. A wild dog had cornered them at the park, and her mama bear instinct took over. Now, she felt the same urge to run to Grace.

Harvey and Melody were close behind as Colleen's feet pounded the old, wooden porch steps. Grace sat up, startled by their presence. Colleen fell on her knees and threw her arms around the girl as Grace sobbed with relief, not because she was found, but because they wanted to find her.

Without hesitation, Grace embraced Colleen, holding on tightly. Melody knelt on the other side of Grace and enveloped both of them. All could see that the girl was okay, and the tears fell as liquid praise.

As Grace felt another set of arms around her, she turned and lunged for Melody, burying her face in her shoulder and weeping. Melody looked up at Colleen, and Colleen locked eyes with her daughter. It was in that moment that Colleen saw Melody was a mama bear, too. *She can be a mother to this child,* Colleen thought. *And she should be.*

There wasn't time for many words then, but the hugs and tears spoke for themselves. The deputies soon came, and an ambulance arrived as a precaution. Then the loving scene was overtaken by sirens and lights, reports and protocol.

At the hospital, the doctors found Grace to be fine physically, although she was exhausted from the hours of wandering. Graciously, the nurses let her stay there in the triage area, just to sleep and to recharge from the ordeal.

Three chairs were pulled close to Grace's bed, and three women watched over her as she slept. They took turns dozing but never left her side.

It was mid-morning when Grace woke up, a little disoriented. Physically, she was forty-five minutes away from Springville, but emotionally, she was a long distance from the fury that had led her there. In both ways, she was close to people who cared for her deeply.

It hadn't taken long for the fire to cool and her heart to settle the night before, after her outburst toward Colleen, but by that point, she was already wandering aimlessly, without any idea of where to go or what to do. She was afraid of being punished for running away and afraid of being rejected by the people she cared about because of her hateful words.

Colleen and Melody let Becky start the talking, and they tried to contain their joy at just seeing Grace's eyelids open. They didn't want to overwhelm her. But Grace reached out and took Melody's hand as Becky spoke gently.

"Grace, we're so glad you're safe. We were very worried about you. How do you feel?" She intentionally spoke for all of them. She had seen just how much Colleen and Melody both loved Grace, too.

"I think I'm fine," Grace said. "Just still tired." Becky didn't have to ask any more questions because Grace let the answers flow like water in a spring. She told them about the woman, about feeling so confused, and about blowing up at Colleen.

Grace looked at Colleen with concern on her face. "After I got so mad, I thought you wouldn't want to keep working with me. I was afraid you would never want to see me again. And that made me more upset."

"Oh, honey," Colleen said, "everybody says things they don't mean sometimes. I forgive you! You're too special for me to throw away our friendship over one little spat."

Grace smiled. She liked hearing that word, *special*. She gripped Melody's hand as if she never wanted to let go. Suddenly, her eyes widened, and she sat up in bed. "Wait! What is today?" she asked, almost panicked.

"It's Wednesday, sweetie," Melody answered, reaching over to stroke her hair. "Why?"

"But your meeting was today, Colleen! What about your meeting? Aren't you supposed to be there now with the producers? Your game show! *What about your game show?*"

"Oh, that. Well, being here was just more important to me," Colleen answered matter-of-factly, with no hint of regret or disappointment.

"You missed it for me?" Grace asked in disbelief. It was difficult for her to comprehend that someone would sacrifice something so important to them just for her.

"Well, of course! I needed to," Colleen replied. She didn't give a drawn-out explanation. The gesture spoke for itself. Grace was important. Someone had finally shown her how valuable she really was.

Chapter Thirty

QUESTIONS

THINGS WERE COMPLICATED FOR A little while. Becky felt she needed to shield Grace from too much excitement, so she postponed the "punishment" indefinitely; and Grace had to take a break from helping Melody with the store. Every day, Grace asked when she could see them again; and every day, Becky told her, "Soon." She hated to restrict the visits, but Becky wanted time to keep a close eye on Grace and to make sure she wouldn't turn into an Olympic sprinter again at the first sign of emotional distress. Melody called Becky every day to check on her.

Grace talked to the counselor at Oak Grove often, and she began working through what had caused her to run away. Each conversation brought out some new pain Grace had forgotten was there, and she allowed herself to relive and understand the abandonment and loss that were her reality. But as if the pain was water and the talking was heat, the hurt seemed to evaporate more with each conversation. Sometimes, Becky sat in on the sessions and asked questions of her own, trying to better understand the girl's motivation.

"Grace, can I ask why you went to Mr. Hartman's house that night? I've been wondering. Why there?" she asked.

"I guess I just like it there. It's a special place, and being there made me feel special. I like feeling that way." She looked Becky in the eyes. "He didn't know me as the poor orphan. He just liked me for me."

Becky spent almost a week paying attention to Grace above her normal duties at the home. They talked a lot and enjoyed time together, while Becky tried to decide what was really best for Grace without Grace knowing there was anything to decide.

There were processes to be followed. She couldn't just hand her over, no matter how ideal the situation seemed. But after several discussions with Melody, Becky was almost positive that she knew what needed to be done. Grace could finally be in a permanent, loving home, cared for by someone who would do anything to make sure Grace was happy.

"It won't be easy," Becky had said to Melody more than once.

"I know," Melody replied each time. "That's okay."

Becky came to the decision that she would do everything she could to help Melody complete the state requirements and get her foster parent license before Christmas. The adoption process could soon follow. She just had to decide how to approach the subject with Grace and when was a safe time to tell her. She was confident that Melody wouldn't back out, but she didn't know whether Grace should find out about her intentions now or closer to when it could actually happen. And there was the matter of whether Grace would agree to the arrangement.

Becky sat in her stuffy office, with papers and files scattered all around her. She pushed her short hair behind her ear and stared at the mess as she processed for the thousandth time what it all meant. Each file represented a person, a young life with unimaginable potential.

The papers in front of her represented impressionable minds and pliable hearts just waiting to be guided and molded into the version of themselves they were meant to be. More than black letters on white paper, the documents and folders she possessed represented unrealized dreams of a family and a place to belong. They represented a child waiting, some hopefully and some without any hope, for something that might never happen.

Becky regularly prayed over each paper file. Some of them showed the signs—small, ringed water spots where her tears had fallen. On the days when she became so overwhelmed with grief, it wasn't just for the children in her care. She grieved also for all the people who missed out on loving those children and being loved by them.

Becky picked up the phone to call Melody.

"I think we should tell her soon," Becky said. "And I think your mother should be there, too. Of course, that's up to you. But it was her project that brought you two together."

"It was more than that!" Melody exclaimed, almost too overwhelmed with joy to speak.

"I know," Becky said, smiling. "So, when do you think we can get together?"

"I have the perfect time in mind. What about after the grand opening of *Grace & Lavender*? She hasn't seen the store all set up. I can't wait to show her. She's going to be so happy! I just hope she's happy about us becoming a family."

"It will work out, Melody," Becky reassured. "'All things work together for good.'"[7]

---

7 Romans 8:28

Chapter Thirty-One

THE ANSWERS

THE WHOLE FAMILY SHOWED UP for the grand opening of *Grace & Lavender*. Michael and Kimberly surprised Melody by taking time off work to be there, to celebrate with her and to help if needed. Melody was excited to see her niece, too.

"Prairie Catherine Hill! Come here to Aunt Mel!" she squealed, scooping the child in her arms and spinning around. They let Prairie pick out a bar and hand Aunt Mel the money, so she was officially the first customer.

"I'm so proud of you, sis," Michael told Melody, even as he wrapped an arm around her neck and delivered a gentle noogie to the top of her head. "This place looks amazing! Your displays and signage and the packaging. It's all really beautiful." He picked up an oval-shaped bar of fragrant lemongrass soap and studied it. "You've done a great job," he said.

She hugged her twin tightly at the compliments. Having his approval and support meant the world to her.

Jason was there for part of the morning, too, taking lots of pictures of the grand opening event. After he snapped several shots of the Hill family in front of the store, with the new white lettering on the window, Harvey said, "Let me get one of the two of you," as he motioned for Melody and Jason to pose for the camera.

Jason and Melody looked at one another bashfully, then he put his arm around her waist and pulled her close to him. They both smiled as naturally as they had for their prom photo so many years before, and Melody had to admit it to herself—she enjoyed being so close to him.

It wasn't long before the customers started trickling in, a few here and there at first, then more around the lunch hour. By mid-afternoon, there was a noticeable decrease in inventory on the shelves and the white cloth-covered tables spread around the store.

Colleen and Harvey stayed with her all day, even after the others had left. They relished in seeing Melody so happy about the first day's success.

"We've had a steady stream of customers all day!" Melody said. "The first day has gone even better than I hoped."

"I know! I think just about everybody that had lunch at the Soda Shop stopped in here. And most of them bought something!" Colleen said.

Melody took advantage of the break from customers to check her phone. "Guess what! I just got an email from a shop owner in Ashe County. He's agreed to stock some of my products! And he has three stores!" Melody was on top of the world.

"Oh, and Mama," Melody said, not hinting at anything important, "I got another email you should know about. I want you to read this one. Daddy, you come on over here, too." She had been waiting for the right moment all day.

Colleen took the glasses from the top of her head and put them on as Melody handed over the phone, and Harvey joined them from across the store.

"Read it out loud," Melody encouraged.

Colleen began reading.

Dear Ms. Hill,

Thank you for your call to our production team on behalf of your mother, Mrs. Colleen Hill, explaining her absence from our call-back meetings in Raleigh last week. The details you provided were passed along to me; and in light of her extraordinary circumstances, we would be honored for your mother to come be a contestant on our show—no further interviews required.

I will be reaching out to her with a personal invitation soon. And, I must say, based on the application she submitted to us, I am truly looking forward to meeting her. She sounds like a very interesting lady!

Sincerely,

Rodney J. Vaughn

Colleen's eyes were wide and her mouth open as she finished the letter.

"See, Mama," Melody said with a grin. "Even Rodney Vaughn can tell how interesting you are, and he hasn't even met you in person yet. Everybody knows how interesting Colleen Hill is!"

"I can't believe you called them! I'm going to be on the show! Oh, Melody, this is wonderful. Thank you," Colleen said, throwing her arms around her daughter in a happy embrace. "I just thought the chance was gone!"

"I couldn't stand the thought of you missing your opportunity," Melody said. "I know how badly you've wanted it."

Colleen hugged Harvey, too, who was grinning from ear to ear.

She was obviously excited, but her mother's reaction lacked the dancing and jumping around that Melody had expected. Colleen was usually more theatrical in her celebrations.

"This is what you wanted, right, Mama?" Melody asked.

"Oh, yes! I'm very happy, dear. So happy! I sincerely appreciate what you've done," Colleen answered. "It's just that, with all the good stuff we have going on in our family, the game show doesn't seem quite as exciting as it used to. I have even better things to be excited about." Melody hugged her mother once more.

"Plus, I've been doing some thinking," Colleen said. She spoke as if she had a confession to make. "When I stand before the Lord in Heaven, it won't matter that I wrote a cookbook or was on a game show." She was resolute. "I think it's time for me to focus more on things that will matter in eternity."

"But there's lots of ways to do that, Mama!" The daughter who once chastised her for doing too much now saw value in the way her mother had approached life. Somewhere along the way, their philosophies had converged. "What was that you said? Something about not stopping to smell the roses when there is a whole garden to sniff?"

Colleen laughed. "I guess you're right, sweetie. I don't have to stop pursuing all my interests. But from now on, I'm going to take more time to consult the Gardener first."

Melody was grateful for a light-hearted moment. The day was winding down, and she was getting nervous. Grace would be there soon.

So many questions ran through her brain. *What do I say to her? How will she react? What if it's too overwhelming for her?*

Becky arrived with Grace half an hour before the shop closed, as planned. When they pulled up and parked in front of the store on

Main Street, Grace sat in the car for a moment, staring at the name of the shop on the window. The lettering of the decal Melody purchased was beautiful, and the feeling Grace had seeing her own name in big, fancy script was amazing. The sign was so professional. Grace realized the store was a real and official business, and her name was on the front of it.

But that's not just my name, Grace thought, still clutching the door handle inside the car. She was frozen with the realization that had just hit her. *Names have meaning, and mine means something good.* She remembered Colleen's words the day she had given the homeless man money. *A favor that isn't deserved,* she thought. *That's what Colleen showed, by staying with me and missing her game show meeting! And Melody, by teaching me to make soap. And Mrs. Johnson, all this time, making sure I was taken care of, even though I wasn't very nice to her sometimes.*

Stepping out of the car and onto the sidewalk, Grace's heart was full, thinking of the kindness of three very special women. Her next thought was an image of the cross that hung on the wall behind the pulpit at Springville Community Christian Church; and for the first time, she really understood the meaning of her name.

Melody was waiting at the door to greet Becky and Grace. She could barely contain her excitement. "What do you think, Grace?" she said, ushering them in. She wanted to grab Grace in a hug and hold on for a long time, but instead, she put her arm around her shoulder and gave a little squeeze.

"I think it's perfect!" Grace answered, as she turned in all directions to take in the store. She breathed in deeply. "And it smells so good in here!"

"It's so good to see you, Grace!" Colleen walked toward the girl and hugged her. Grace hugged back tightly.

"It's good to see you, too," Grace said. Then seeing Harvey standing behind her, she surprised him with a big bear hug, for which he was grateful.

Both Colleen and Harvey had transitioned quickly from the idea of having another daughter to the idea of having another granddaughter, and they couldn't be happier.

They let Grace inspect the store, then step back into the kitchen to see if anything had changed there. Becky exchanged hugs and handshakes with the other adults. A customer came in, and Grace watched Melody point out all the scents and shapes of soap available to purchase. It was hard to believe that the store she last saw practically empty was a working business now. Melody let Grace be the cashier, showing her how to enter the information into the tablet and calculate the total. At 5:00 p.m., Melody let Grace turn the *Open* sign to *Closed* and lock the door.

Grace was content and happy, but she sensed nervousness from the adults around her. Then with four smiling faces turned toward her, in the middle of *Grace & Lavender*, the news came.

"Grace, we want to talk to you about something," Becky started. Usually when Grace heard those words, bad news followed. But these smiling faces didn't seem to forebear bad news. The conversation that followed was better to Grace than every birthday and Christmas combined, and it ended with, "Grace, how do you feel about all this?"

Grace didn't answer. She hadn't taken her eyes off Melody since she realized what was going on. She could hardly believe what she was hearing—that Melody wanted to be her foster mother and hopefully adopt her, that it would take a few months, but that soon she would be going to live with Melody, if that's what she wanted.

Grace didn't answer with words at first, but she shot toward Melody with arms extended, wrapping them around her neck in a heartfelt embrace. The teenager let herself be a little girl again, collecting from that single hug all the ones she had secretly longed for throughout the years.

"I can't believe this is happening!" Grace sounded off joyfully, and Melody's heart overflowed with love and, at last, with purpose.

Colleen stood close by, ready to jump in and join the hugging when the time was right. She watched Melody stroke Grace's long, black hair. She wouldn't trade being there to witness that moment for an appearance on all the game shows in the world. She was right where she wanted to be.

It's amazing what love does, Colleen thought, fighting back tears.

She looked around the store, noticing the bunches of long-stemmed purple flowers placed aesthetically throughout. She thought about their abilities to help soothe and heal wounds. She whispered thanks to the Creator. And she soaked up the joy in the room, as love poured out like a lavender ointment to a young girl's soul.

EPILOGUE

MELODY COULDN'T WAIT TO GET inside. A fire was going in the fireplace, and the Christmas tree was completely decorated, except for the star on top, which would be Grace's honor to add. Melody was still reeling from the wild ride that had led her to this point, but she possessed a surreal confidence that it all had been planned long before her first breath.

"Okay, don't open your eyes yet!" Melody said, leading Grace by the hand as she stepped out of the car. The air around her was cold and alive with excitement. The ground underneath her feet was soft with the gift of a rare snow, and so was the gloved hand of her now-official foster mother.

"Okay, you can open them!"

Grace, all bundled up in the new coat and hat Melody had bought for her, stood frozen at first, not with cold, but with bewilderment.

"What . . . but . . . why are we here?"

"This is our new home, Grace! It's all ours," Melody explained. "It was left to the church in Mr. Hartman's will, and I bought it from them. It's ours! And the money from the sale will go to their youth program. Isn't it wonderful?" Her words had come out fast, but then Melody paused to read the emotion on Grace's face. "I wanted to surprise you with a place I thought would make you happy," she said. "I hope you *are* happy."

Grace & Lavender

Grace stared at the house and the bare apple trees in the front yard, still stiff except for her quick, short breaths. *How could this be?* she thought. She looked at Melody, then back at the house; then she ran away without warning, around the house and to the backyard.

When Melody caught up to her, she was standing perfectly still, staring off into the distance. "We're really going to live here?" Grace asked. "Me and you?"

Melody was comforted by Grace's wistful tone. "Me and you, Grace," she answered. "Does that make you happy?"

Grace spoke from her heart as the haze lifted off the tops of the Blue Ridge Mountains as if they were offering themselves to her. "I can't think of anything better."

They were her mountains now. This was her home now. This was her life now. And it was more than enough.

The End

As of late 2017, there were over 435,000 children in foster care in the United States. Over 110,000 were in immediate need of adoptive homes. About 20,000 age out of foster care every year, unprepared to live on their own and unsupported.

Prayerfully consider contacting a local foster care and adoption agency near you to find out how you can serve a child in need of a family.

In Western North Carolina, you can contact Crossnore School & Children's Home, whose mission is to grow healthy futures for children and adults by providing a Christian sanctuary of hope and healing. To learn more, visit them at www.crossnore.org.

For more information about
Heather Norman Smith
&
Grace & Lavender
please visit:

www.heathernormansmith.com
@HNSblog
www.facebook.com/heathernormansmith
www.instagram.com/heathernormansmith

For more information about
AMBASSADOR INTERNATIONAL
please visit:

www.ambassador-international.com
@AmbassadorIntl
www.facebook.com/AmbassadorIntl

If you enjoyed this book, please consider leaving us a review on
Amazon, Goodreads, or our website.

DEC 1 8 2019

Made in the USA
Columbia, SC
10 August 2019